POLAR BEARS
IN THE KITCHEN

Joan Leslie Woodruff

Polar Bears in the Kitchen

Published by Wheatmark®
610 East Delano Street, Suite 104
Tucson, Arizona 85705 U.S.A.
www.wheatmark.com

International Standard Book Number: 978-1-60494-293-4
Library of Congress Control Number: 2009927411

Author contact info.

Chapter One

I crouched, sat straight, placed feet flat on floor, leaned to the right, leaned to the left, leaned on an elbow, perched precariously on the edge, acknowledged defeat and stood up. Chairs could not possibly be designed for more discomfort than these. Arching my back, I stretched tall to release some of the ache, then walked to Dana's hospital bed. She looked peacefully at rest. Upon each in-breath, her entire rib cage expanded until her stomach rose, and I worried she might be trying to get more oxygen. The hospice doctor, a fiftyish woman who wore brightly colored long dresses, cowboy boots and velvet vests, assured me this was normal.

I worried anyway and wondered if Dana would open her eyes, at least once more.

"Cousin? Do you know I'm here?" I asked. Picking up her left hand, I examined her fingers. Still warm.

"Your neighbors miss you," I said, and for an instant her eyebrows responded. I almost expected her eyelids to raise up.

"Time for her repositioning," a voice whispered from the doorway.

"I'll go for a walk," I replied.

The hospice nurse and her aid entered. They moved silently.

Like ghosts.

Or angels.

Always respectful and gentle.

Always quiet. As if their slightest movements or most minimal sounds might disturb their patients, all who would die, perhaps today, tonight, tomorrow. Certainly within the week. Hospice units in hospitals were atypical. The people who worked here had similarities not usually seen anywhere else: Their faces bright like stars in a night sky, terminally filled with kindness. Their temperaments compassionate. Not one harsh personality. Not one inconsiderate nurse or surly aid. Only silently caring, smiling, present. Ghosts or angels. I hadn't decided.

How did hospitals find all these special creatures, as unique as snowflakes. And how did they keep them, year after year, where all who came in would leave one day soon in a body bag?

"I think she can hear me," I offered before leaving.

The nurse smiled and nodded. "Of course she can hear you. She knows you are here."

I studied nurse and helper. More angelic smiles.

"Her eyebrows twitched," I added, "when I spoke, just before you arrived."

"I'm sure she was trying to comfort you," the nurse whispered.

"I'll be in the cafeteria," I said.

"We'll come and get you if anything changes."

I tried to smile. My facial muscles simply sagged. The nurse said Dana was trying to comfort me. Comfort me? Cancer finally defeated my once strong resilient cousin. End stage cancer, her doctors all agreed. While I made my way to the cafeteria sensations of a static world overcame me.

Time wasn't like a train.

It did not run on a track.

Not forward, not backward.

No history. No future. Just the moment. Such a terrible thing, to be ensnared within a painful moment. Like being trapped inside a jar.

Aimless, without direction or intention of getting anywhere, I put my feet into motion and simply followed my face. Down long corridors, past working departments and busy hospital offices, into and out of patient care units, through exit doors, traveling the length of sidewalks which always seemed to return to the same lobby entrance. Eventually I arrived at the counter of a mini mart. Placing a pint of orange juice on the counter -- although I hadn't realized I'd wanted orange juice -- I heard the woman ask for money.

"I'm sorry?"

"That will be two dollars and eleven cents," the woman repeated.

After handing her several dollar bills, I exited without waiting for my change. I didn't return immediately to Dana's room. There was a narrow garden outside her room window and I'd seen other people in this garden. They cried, or stared in disbelief, or simply sat with faces too vacant for description.

A large dove visited the garden, an incongruent event because doves are not often seen in the middle of Albuquerque. They are plentiful in the outlying areas, but not in the city, and doves are not solitaire birds, they live in coveys. I wondered what happened to this ones covey.

I picked a concrete bench not too far from Dana's window. I could see her from here. Soon as I sat down the dove appeared. It perched directly across from me on a tree limb, watching me, as if knowing something I did not know and wanting to tell me what that something might be. When the garden door opened and a new visitor arrived, the dove took flight and disappeared.

November has its share of cold evenings, but day temperatures tend toward pleasant. Today was very pleasant. Most of the tree leaves had lost their bright autumn hues and now resembled coffee colored pieces of paper, majestically floating when a breeze picked up, or scattering like skittish sheep for no apparent purpose.

When several weeping visitors arrived I hastily vanished back inside the hospital.

* * *

Nestled comfortably in the middle of the hospice unit, a cozy kitchen, a dinning area and a television lounge offered snacks, juice, coffee, movies, books, newspapers, daily news shows, and various other undertakings meant to provide us -- the family of the dying -- as much normalcy as possible. And, although there were several signs on the wall which clearly stated "*No sleeping allowed*" I often came over here to do just that. Sleep. Twice someone had covered me with a blanket when I broke the rules and slumbered.

While pouring hot water and dropping in a tea bag, Dana's hospice doctor entered. She offered her cup and I filled it with steaming water from the same pot. She stirred in hot cocoa mix before addressing me. "How are you managing?"

"Like ice cream on a hot spoon," I said.

"Is that good or bad?"

"I've never felt more lost, hopeless, grief stricken, sad, mad, tired, bewildered. I guess that isn't good, is it?"

"Would you like to see our grief counselor?"

I shook my head.

"Shall we go in and check her?"

"Sure," I said, following the velvet vested woman into my cousin's room.

Lifting the blanket from Dana's feet, the doctor inspected them.

"A bit cool," the doctor said. "No discoloration, yet. The coolness is a change. I'll check on her again before I leave tonight."

I'd learned a lot about dying from the hospice doctors and nurses. Her body actually knew it was dying, and the need for nutrition and hydration slowed a great deal during the last few months. The evening Dana's doctor told me to bring her here, she was still walking to the bathroom. The second day her legs collapsed when she tried to get out of bed. That evening she asked me for a drink of juice, but she could not swallow the liquid. A few hours later her sleep deepened, and she had not been awake since. The last thing she'd said was: "I know you will miss me. I won't be far away."

I wished she would open her eyes. Frequently I spoke to her. The doctors and nurses advised me not to do that. They said every time I began talking to Dana, she put every ounce of her energy into hanging on to a few more hours of life because somewhere deep in her mind, she believed that's what I needed her to do. It is what I needed. I was selfish and worried about myself. I could not stand this. What would I do? She was practically my only family. We had our niece, Sandy. I wished Sandy were here but she'd returned to Memphis earlier this year and was working at St. Jude Children's Hospital. Sandy needed this new job. She could not take a chance of losing it by taking a leave of absence so soon after being hired.

Every few minutes I checked Dana's feet, obsessed with worry, frantic about what I would see when I lifted the blanket. Nothing really changed until her doctor stopped in before she left at eleven. She nodded at me.

"Won't be long now. Splotches are getting larger. You should say everything you need to say. Would you like me to call the hospital chaplain?"

"Yes," I said, not knowing why. Dana was as spiritual as most modern day American Indians. I doubted she'd ever been to a formal church, at least not that I was aware. Still, it seemed the right thing to do.

When the doctor left I pulled Dana's blanket back off her feet and didn't need to touch them. The mottling effect appeared exactly as the hospice staff described. Dana's feet were the color of a pinkish purple popsicle. Feet and legs would grow cooler, and eventually there would be discoloration of the toes, then the feet, and it would creep into the lower legs. Perhaps there would be discoloration in the hands, too, although death usually occurred before this happened. That is what they'd told me. I thought I would be prepared.

Collapsing into the difficult chair beside her bed, I held her hand. The fingers did not fold over my palm like they'd done the previous day. I folded her fingers and squeezed her hand. Tears swelled across my face and dripped off my chin like a broken faucet. A sense of puzzlement overcame me and I could not think.

"Life is hard." The words stumbled around through my mouth. Nothing anyone could do. Dana was going away. For each long treacherous second of suffering I now must endure, I knew she was already gone. Breathing would continue. Perhaps an hour, or even several hours. The lungs kept trying to keep the body alive, it was some weird twist of biology that this is how things ended. The limbs were not needed, and the body shut off blood supply to them first. Gradually, the vital organs would be selected, one by one, the least important getting shut down first. Finally, the lungs would cease to pull oxygen and the heart would stop.

Nothing prepared me. Not all the books the hospice staff offered me to read: kindly worded paragraphs detailing the final journey; not the words they shared; not the fears I tried to smother and pretend were within my control.

My suffering peaked at midnight until a numbness settled over my mind. Its purpose, surely, kept me from going insane. I could not stop crying. I wanted to die.

At approximately ten minutes past midnight Dana passed away.

All timelines ceased.

Nothing existed in any direction.

Not up, nor down.

Not east, nor west.

Please help me ran through my head until I grew lightheaded.

The night nurse presented papers for me to sign. She seemed all the while to be saying something. Words probably meant to comfort. I watched her mouth move. My ears did not hear.

I returned to Dana's room and immediately panicked. Her bed was empty. In her place there was a plastic bag. I opened it and poured out the contents: Dana's nightgowns, her favorite sandals, hairbrush, toothbrush, toothpaste, face cream, shampoo, reading glasses, and the funny little hat she sometimes wore. Suddenly it occurred to me, Dana had retrieved each one of these items, packed them, brought them here. These were the leftovers from my cousin's life. Remainders of Dana. All that she believed she would need during her hospice stay.

Hospice stay?

How often did those who checked in get to check out?

My thoughts rested on her reading glasses. What had she wanted to read? I wasn't aware she'd wanted to read anything, but why else did she bring her reading glasses? And her toothbrush and toothpaste?

Good grief! She was dying. This was so like Dana, wanting to be presentable, even if her only visitors were body collectors from a funeral home. Before I left during the early hours that morning, Dana's room was cleaned and someone else had taken her place.

Daylight loitered at least two hours away and all that illuminated darkness around my car were dim parking lot lamps. Once inside I started the engine and cranked up the heater. The temperature was at or below freezing and my warm breath fogged the cold-cold windshield. I let the car idle for a few minutes before heading for home.

I thought about the past few years. I'd sold my small ranch in central New Mexico and, after a lot of pestering from Dana, built a comfortable home near her small adobe north of Santa Fe. We were always busy. We made our own clay and designed unique pottery which we sold in local galleries. We spent part of every autumn working the property repairing fences, trimming trees, burning brush, and maintaining both homes. Dana's unusual neighbors were always up to something exciting and strange. When I arrived my small family added to this menagerie. My additions were probably more odd, more interesting, and more unique than even the greatest of imaginations could imagine.

Bailey wasn't really odd. She was a dog. Rudy and I found her several years earlier. She wandered abandoned in traffic on a busy street. We rescued her. Rudy was odd. He found me in an animal shelter when he appeared there as a puppy. Although he never actually was a puppy.

Rudy is a Spirit Wolf.

I think of him as a *ghost in the rainbow*.

He is not a living animal, yet he does possess remarkable powers and strength. Never truly of this earth, Rudy is a magnificent creature. He roams the sky like a phantom, and when he chooses, he jumps on rainbows and races across the Heavens. When he leaves I have no idea where he goes, and when he visits, I am clueless as to how long he will stay.

"He's an Angel," Dana always said.

I didn't know about the angel part. Rudy killed Haggis.

Snow floated, now, beyond my headlight beams.

Swirling and twirling.

Skittering perilously.

Like crazy drunken rabbits on the run.

Haggis, never up to being human, was now *rabbit*.

One summer morning Dana ran across her field to my house and woke me. "Rudy is chasing Haggis around the yard," she yelled.

"What?!"

"You gotta get up and see this. It is the funniest thing."

"Haggis is dead. Rudy tore his throat out in front of the Navajo police up in the mountains above Gallup. That was years ago!"

"I know," Dana laughed. "And now Rudy's chasing him all over the yard. I think it's Haggis's curse. You'll see what I mean. He is going to be running for a very long time."

Wearing my pajamas, I followed Dana outside.

A rabbit with Haggis's head was racing helter-skelter around the yard with the massive white wolf nipping at his tail.

It was grotesque and ugly. Funny and wild.

"Haggis is a rabbit," I said.

"Rip him up!" Dana yelled out. Rudy grabbed his tail and tore a plug. The Haggis headed rabbit squealed and hopped in circles.

"What is it?" I asked.

Dana shrugged. "Haggis was evil. He cut off his own child's head. He butchered his wife. He tried to kill you. He hacked Rudy into pieces with an ax. He didn't know Rudy wasn't really a dog. The Spirit Wolf leaped from the clouds and tore out his throat, that was only the beginning of Haggis's curse."

CHAPTER TWO

D riving toward my house two things were immediately obvious.
My kitchen lights were on.

Mule was standing near the kitchen bay window spying on whoever was in my kitchen.

Throwing the door wide, with Mule following so close on my heels I could feel his breath, the first words out of my mouth were "What the ... ?"

Coffee grounds spilled out across my once spotless central counter top, the coffee maker was on, the empty carafe was on the hot plate, cups were scattered everywhere, and a blasting noise from my living room came from the television.

I turned to fix my stare square on Mule, and he backed out of the kitchen. I closed the door and noticed he'd resumed his little post listening beside the window. While heading down the hall to my living room I was greeted by Bailey. Dropping to my knees I hugged her, burying my face in her doggy smelling fur. "We lost our Dana," I whispered. Bailey whined, and I hoped she understood.

Looking up, colorful cartoon characters raced about my flat screen. Kopeki sat on the blanket he always used from Dana's house. Obviously, he went over there and got it, and brought it here. Sam occupied the chair Dana always sat in when she visited.

"What are you doing?" I barked.

"This television is much larger than Missy's." Sam glanced at me across the large room. The grin which spread across his face seemed to touch both his ears. Sam always called Dana "Missy". Of all the people she'd ever known, I believed this elderly fossil of a cowboy was one of her favorite. And Mule was definitely her favorite animal. I'd have to remember that, because with Dana gone, I was it. This menagerie of odd neighbors would invade my space as frequently as they had invaded Dana's. I would have to learn patience.

"This is a very good kachina." Kopeki commented about my flat screen.

"Dana just died!"

Sam switched off the television and they both stood and dropped their shoulders.

"We knew already," Sam offered.

At that moment Nakani appeared from my hallway.

"What are you doing?"

"You have more clothes than Dana."

"Dana is gone." I repeated. "And you invade my home. Mess up my kitchen. Watch my television. And pilfer through my closets." I began wondering why I had to put up with them on this morning when I did not feel like breathing.

"No." Nakani's expression was of true surprise. "I just saw her."

I spun and faced Nakani. "You were at the hospice?"

"I saw her out there." Nakani pointed toward the hills where the ancient pueblo ruins scattered across the land. "She's a powerful Kachina. I always said that." Snapping her fingers and emitting a whistle, she continued. "What about hi'anyi? Why is she the only live person I ever knew who could do that? I think it's Magic. That's why. I knew it. Skipping hi'anyi. Like she's so special. Like rules don't matter."

I almost felt sorry for Nakani. If ghosts could panic, she was panicking.

Hi'anyi was the journey, according to the ancients, that a person must follow after death of the body, before reaching the peaceful place where they wanted to rest. Hi'anyi encompassed four days, during which those left behind in life would chase roadrunners back and forth across the grave. All those bird tracks would, according to the ancient's, confuse witches and other evil spirits, so that the witches and evil spirits could not interfere with the deceased spirit's arrival at that desired place of peace. Evidently Dana jumped across those four days and arrived at her place of peace, and now she was wrecking Nakani's peace. All this only hours after her death.

"Why would she be there?" I asked. "She isn't an ancient."

"Well, she was there."

"What was she doing?"

Nakani stiffened a bit. "She was painting over my pots."

Nakani had a long history of painting designs over Dana's pottery designs. "Dana just died, and you're telling me her Spirit hurried over here, first thing, to paint over your pottery designs?"

Nakani frowned, scrunching her eyebrows into a distress expression. "That's what she did." Nakani clicked her tongue. "Pretty sneaky. I told her so."

"I can't believe this. And I can't believe you are all here. Why don't you go to Dana's house? That's where you've always gone."

"It's much warmer here," Kopeki called out from the background where he was eavesdropping.

"How d'you know the freaking difference between warm and warmer? None of you wear a freaking coat, even when there's three freaking feet of snow on the ground."

"You want us to leave, Missy's cousin?" Sam asked.

I turned to see the pathetic faces of Dana's neighbors. I did not know why she loved these old ghosts so much. They annoyed the heck out of me. "I hope you aren't going to be calling me Missy's cousin, Sam. You always called me Myra. I am Myra Whitehawk."

"The Whitehawk Woman was the best trickster ever," Kopeki winked.

"She is still the best tricky tricker." Nakani clicked her tongue again. "Now she's probably going to be even better. She's going to mess up everything I make. She's going to paint over all my pots. Now she can find them. Even the ones that are hundred of years in the ground." With that, Nakani tore out of the house and disappeared over the distant pueblo hill.

"We will call you Myra-the-cousin-for-Whitehawk Woman," Kopeki offered.

"No you won't. You'll call me Myra. Like you always have. By the way, where's Ben?"

"At the killing ground," Sam said.

"What's he doing there?"

"Breaking pottery."

"Whose pottery?"

"Dana's pottery." Sam shrugged, as if he didn't understand why I'd ask such a stupid redundant question. For the ancients when a person died their worldly possession, things like pottery, were taken to what was called the killing ground, and destroyed. Perhaps the belief being this freed any trapped energy from those items, and this extra energy aided any transition.

"Never mind," I said, turning to my dog. "Bailey," I kneeled and looked into her eyes, "you stay here. Keep an eye on them." Sam and Kopeki smiled innocently.

Wanting nothing more than sleep, I dragged myself down my hallway and discovered Nakani had rummaged through all my drawers. They were half open and everything was a mess. Inside my walk in closet, many of my best clothes were hanging askew on their hangers. Nakani had been trying them on. I wondered if she'd done this with Dana's clothes. Of course she had. Dana was gone. Now I was their captive.

Pulling fresh jeans and a warm fleece shirt over my tired body, I donned winter boots and left through the back French doors, avoiding more ridiculous conversation with my cousin's neighbors.

Sam died less than twenty years earlier. I wasn't sure when Nakani died. About eleven hundred years ago, Dana had guessed. Kopeki was much more youthful. He died about nine hundred years ago. And Ben? Who knew. At his time of death he was a child of about ten. He was still ten years old. Ben and Mule were my favorites. They'd stolen my heart, the same way they stole Dana's heart. Mule was killed when a vehicle hit him around the time Dana bought this property. He'd wandered about, not understanding that he was actually a ghost mule, and Dana adopted him. She didn't know, at that time, that he wasn't really alive. She actually loaded him into a horse trailer and took him on trail rides. Evidently, Mule enjoyed trail rides. I always wondered how she figured out all her neighbors were ghosts. She never told me. In fact, she never told me they were ghosts. She let me figure it out myself.

Rudy was the clue. Ben directed me to him, told me he was the best puppy, and I adopted Rudy. When Haggis killed Rudy, I thought my heart would burst from the grief. That's when I discovered Rudy wasn't a puppy. Rudy is an ancient Wolf Spirit, and he was never a live animal. Rudy is kind of like an Angel. Or an alien. Or something. I'm not sure. All I know is he is my best friend. And I absolutely adore him. I wondered where he was now. I wished he'd fly out of the sky and sit beside me.

I picked a path Mule traveled along when he visited Rooster and the Happy Hens everyday. While I walked Mule tagged along with his big mule head hung low near the ground. I thought of jumping up on his back and riding, allowing him to pick our destination, and was about to swing myself up when a fireball dropped from the sky. It hit the ground near us and Mule said "Phwphwphw."

The Wolf Spirit leaped from the fireball seconds before it sped off skyward again. I grabbed his big wolf ears and kissed his forehead. "I missed you, buddy," I said. "I wish you'd been here. Our Dana has gone."

Rudy metamorphosed into a blur of dust, and from the dust a dove appeared. It was the same dove I'd seen every day outside Dana's window. The dove faded and Rudy once again sat before me, studying my face.

"You knew Dana died," I whispered. "You were the dove in the garden."

Rudy jumped to his feet and began trotting off. I swung onto Mule's back, and Mule galloped to keep pace with the wolf.

Prayer sticks lined the trail when we reached a hilltop. Mule halted and Rudy climbed a large boulder which blocked our path. I jumped down and crawled upon the rock, too. Once on top, I balanced carefully, holding a handful of Rudy's fur, and gasped when I realized what we were observing. From the crest of this hill and the top of this boulder, we had a direct visual of Dana's little adobe. She would love this place. Perhaps she'd always known about it's existence, but we'd never been here. It was peaceful and omniscient, with a 360 degree view of the world. And Dana's beloved little house sat in the small valley slightly beneath the most remarkable view of this area I'd ever seen.

Now I knew why Ben placed prayer sticks along the trail, leading us up to this point.

I had objected to her choice of cremation. She insisted. She believed dust to dust, ash to ash. She did not want to be buried in the ground with tons of soil smothering her memory. She wanted to be scattered in the wind. I had no idea where that perfect place could be, and she'd never suggested a place. Now I had found it, or rather Ben had found it. I would bring Dana's ashes here, and from the top of this rock I would liberate my cousin from this earth.

CHAPTER THREE

Thanksgiving passed and Christmas was a few days away. Dana's absence would surely mean this would become the saddest Christmas of my life. I wondered where she was off to? Roaming the universe or visiting places around this planet that she'd always wanted to see, but did not live long enough to make the journey? Although Nakani swore she'd seen my cousin, I seldom believed Nakani's histrionics. Why did Kopeki, Nakani, Ben, Mule, the Happy Hens, and Rooster insist on remaining earthbound? I was not a philosopher and never delved into deep spiritual deliberations which might shed light on this subject.

This day was for shopping. I drove and Bailey sat shotgun while we traveled home from Santa Fe. Our mission had included purchasing a couple hundred pounds of corn for the little ghost chickens, a hundred pounds of sweet treat molasses and grain mixture for Mule, six pounds of coffee for which Kopeki and Sam consumed the lion's share, and a fresh assortment of ceramic paints and glazes to use in Dana's studio.

"Why do they eat, Bailey?"

"Woof." Bailey paused her view out the window to offer agreement on this strange event.

Dana never worried about why. She kept endless supplies of coffee for Sam and Kopeki. Several times a week she sprinkled corn over the pueblo ruins where the Happy Hens and Rooster scratched and cackled, and dined like royalty. She kept Mule's sweet treat in a 50 gallon barrel inside the studio. When he was moody she'd reach in the barrel, retrieve a handful of the stuff, and Mule closed his big brown eyes and nibbled in content until every tidbit was consumed. I always swore he smiled when Dana offered him the molasses treat. I wondered what happened to the snacks they ate? Ghosts produce no waste, and they never drink water. I shrugged this minor mystery off. Dana once told me life was unique, regardless which dimension it existed in at any collection of times. I'd later given the idea some mulling about. If Dana were right, there were no ghosts, and these interesting neighbors actually lived beyond their life experience. They were here because they chose to be here. They could be anywhere but they enjoyed this area. Time was a consideration, Dana often said. Who were we to decide what time meant, or when it began, when it stopped, where it went.

Time was time. Dana said so. End of debate.

Good enough for me. I hated to think deeply about such matters, and Dana's theories usually shielded me from the burden.

I surely missed my cousin and all that confident energy. Nothing stalled her momentum and she seldom complained or worried. If a problem arose, Dana opened the door and headed straight for the solution. For much of my own life when a problem arose, I opened a bottle and headed straight for getting drunk. After my run-in with Haggis while working as a newspaper reporter, I gave up drinking. I could have continued working for the newspaper. Or, because I had stayed sober, I could have gotten my old job back as a biology tech in the university where my ex teaches. I did neither. I sold my place and moved in with Dana until my house was completed across the field from her simple adobe. Probably why I remained sober. Dana was a rare personage. She lacked addictions. I cannot think of one thing in her life that she wasn't willing to do without. Well, maybe I could think of a few: Me, our niece and Bailey; Mule and Ben; Kopeki and Sam; Nakani, the Happy Hens and Rooster. And of course, my Rudy. But things like caffeine, cigarettes, alcohol, narcotics, chocolate, or excess food. Dana did not crave these and she did not miss them.

"You get drunk because you give yourself permission," Dana once told me.

"So what, I just refuse to give myself permission?" I argued.

"That's pretty much it," she'd said. And then she had turned and walked off to busy herself with something useful.

I thought about what she said. She was correct. No one poured alcohol down my throat. I got drunk because I took the first drink.

I considered getting drunk these days. Ever since Dana discovered her cancer, my escape from that news revolved around whether or not I could get drunk enough to make it all go away. Loneliness was the worst. I'd discussed my loneliness with our niece, Sandy. She, too, missed Dana terribly. She wanted me to phone her when I began to feel lonely. If I did that, I'd have to live with the phone in my ear. Loneliness tagged along with me like my shadow.

As I pulled into my driveway Bailey fussed to get out. We always used Dana's old GMC truck to pick up the feed supply, and the passenger door did not open from outside. I stopped and crawled out. Bailey bounded across the bench seat, onto the gravel and raced off over the nearest hill. I shrugged, crawled back into the GMC and drove on to my workshop. That's where we always stored the feed stash, Mule's saddle, our extra pottery supplies, tools, stuff which didn't fit anywhere else. I unloaded the feed bags, stacked them neatly, then headed for my house. While I crossed the yard my eyes rested on the empty little adobe across the half acre field. Dana left all her property to me, and all her cash to our niece. Dana's cash was invested into a retirement portfolio, and some firm in California handled the investments. I knew it was more than a few dollars. I was proud she'd left this to Sandy, who might one day need the money. Our niece had a psychology doctorate and a good job. But she'd suffered a horrific brain injury when she was seventeen. Her mother passed away and Sandy did not have anyone other than me to fall back on if the old injury brought new problems. Head trauma almost always promised residual effects.

As for me, my ranch house and property in central New Mexico was a good investment. I sold it for enough to build a modern home here, and still have a modest chunk of cash earning interest in the bank. I seldom spent more than my monthly interest check. And both Dana and I always earned a few hundred a month off our gallery pieces. She had more pottery in galleries around the state than I did, and now those checks would come to me, too.

"Whoa!" Something flashed across Dana's yard, disappearing behind our ceramic studio before I could see much more than a blur. Probably a small animal, I wasn't particularly worried, but decided to check it out. When I reached the corner of her adobe I spotted Mule standing guard. The Haggis headed rabbit crouched in the corner between house and back porch. Mule showed it a well aimed hoof each time it tried to move.

Rudy snarled, trotting around the corner of one wall, Bailey close on his flanks. They sat on either side of Mule and the three studied their prey.

They were torturing the Haggis creature. It was probably their favorite sport.

Haggis deserved his punishment. Dana believed some Great Spirit had beheaded Haggis so he could experience the same suffering he'd caused his own young son. We'd both decided the same Spirit stuck Haggis's head on a rabbit's body as a morbid joke. Rabbits had more enemies than most other animals, and spent their lives running, hiding, and being tortured by an endless group of predators. The Haggis rabbit was retribution by a higher power.

"Rip him up," I said before turning toward home. They usually did, but because the creature was not a life form, it always put itself back together just in time for Rudy to remember its crimes. I imagined the universe was not large enough to hide Haggis from this great white wolf.

I returned home, slipped on my warmest parka and thermal gloves, scooped up a bucket of corn, and hiked out to the old ruins. Rooster and the Happy Hens crowded around my feet, cackling joyfully, while I sprinkled corn for them to dine upon.

The following morning I shivered crawling from the warm bed. My ultra modern automatic energy efficient electric heaters were useless without power. The electricity had gone off at three in the morning, according to my bedroom clock. No snow, yet, but the early morning sky was cluttered with dark weighty clouds. Still wearing flannel pajamas, I donned my parka and wool lined boots then raced over to Dana's woodpile behind the ceramic studio. Thank goodness Dana always prepared for winter during the early summer. I'd helped her split and stack two cords of pinon. She'd had little time to use much of her winter fuel. I gathered an armload and returned home.

My new home was twice as large as Dana's adobe. In fact, we could fit half of Dana's adobe inside my expansive open kitchen and den with its twelve foot ceilings. In the area between my breakfast counter and the expensive dining room table I'd never used, was a large red brick fireplace with a stone hearth. I seldom set a fire here, because the electric heating system kept my house cozy warm regardless how cold it got outdoors.

After laying some of the logs on top of piled kindling, I struck a match and watched the flames creep along the edges of a split pinon. Gradually the flames engulfed the logs, and when they began to burn hot, I closed the fire screen.

"Woof." Bailey let me know she was pleased with the warmth. Using the blanket Kopeki always sat on, I spread it near the hearth and she plopped down, snoring comfortably within a few seconds.

My electric coffee maker was useless, too. I pulled my boots back on and headed for Dana's. Sure enough, she had two stove top percolators. I grabbed both and left before the stuff of her kitchen, which only reminded me she'd never be busy here again, dropped me deeper into my depression.

Luckily I'd taken her advice and put in a gas range and oven. The automatic pilot didn't function without power, but a match worked fine. Filling the smaller carafe top with grounds, I lit the burner and let it percolate. The sounds made by the old fashioned coffee pot, and the delicious slow-boil smell, filled my house. I half expected Sam and Kopeki to show up any moment, but they never did. I set mugs for them, anyway, before filling my cup and sitting on the bench Dana always called my catbird seat. The builder added this to my oversized kitchen. It was a bay window with a huge bench stretching from one side to the other. I could take a catnap, or I could simply sit and enjoy my view of Dana's adobe with the old ruin hills behind.

By now the fireplace sent warmth throughout much of the house, and the fresh coffee soothed my mood. I was probably more depressed than I'd ever been in my life and I didn't know what to do to help myself. I tried to stay active. I continued with all of Dana's chores and I kept up with my own. Yet each day I slipped deeper. I knew this because I lost track of what day it was in the early weeks. Now I was forgetting the month. If Christmas decorations hadn't greeted me when I went into town, I would forget the month.

"Brroowlf!" Bailey wanted to go out. When I opened the door she bounded past while snowflakes blew across my porch and kissed my cheeks. I wondered how long I'd been lost in my thoughts, oblivious to the storm. Already an easy four inches of powder covered the ground. My visibility didn't stretch beyond my immediate yard and all the objects in the distance were gone, as if all that existed was me, the interior of my house, and Bailey's sharp happy barks.

Bailey, due to her golden color, achieved full invisible status. As long as I could hear her, I knew she was okay. But dogs can get lost in a wet snow storm. The moisture hides smells and they don't know where they are at. I considered this and was on the verge of panicking when she brushed past me, stopped in the middle of my spotless kitchen, and shook herself. At least a bushel of snow was suddenly airborne, and for a moment, it seemed the blizzard moved inside.

"Electricity is off, Kiddo," I said. "Can't use the hairdryer to dry your fur. You'll have to sit beside the fire for awhile."

Throwing another log of pinon onto the burning coals, I seated myself on Kopeki's blanket along with Bailey and began brushing her wet coat.

What was to become of us?

Dana decided to find some of her family. She actually showed up at the university where I worked in Socorro. I didn't need to ask who she was. She looked exactly like me if I added about ten years. Not long afterwards she heard from our other cousin, Sandy's mother. And not long after that, Sandy moved to New Mexico. We were all we had after Sandy's mother died. We were a family of three, and we depended on Dana. Dana was our rock, our anchor, our strength.

Sandy buried herself in her work counseling sick children. Many of the children she worked with suffered from terminal illnesses. They'd never reach the age required for a driver's license. I imagined she'd be okay because so many little people needed her help. Who needed me? Who would notice if I fell off the wagon and started drinking again? Who would give a damn?

Somewhere between feeling sorry for myself and a classic slide into a depressed state, the electricity came back online. My ceiling fans resumed their slow cycles, the automatic heaters hissed and buzzed to reset themselves, and the refrigerator condenser hummed steady. Ah, the sounds of modern comforts.

A brief glance at Bailey assured me, she'd be sound asleep for hours. I hastily suited up for the blizzard and the below freezing temperature, then headed over the hills, across the ancient ruins, traveling toward the place where I'd freed Dana's ashes into the wind.

When I arrived, the worst of the blizzard subsided. It required half a dozen efforts before I could climb onto the top of the boulder due to the ice which caked beneath the fresh snow. From the top all I could see were blankets of white stretching in every direction. I wondered why I was here. My eye lashes began to feel like frozen fans waving up and down each time I blinked, and a few times I struggled to inhale. The air was so thick with moisture and ice, the combination tested life. In fact, I was sure I was the only idiot life form sitting atop a rock in the middle of nowhere in the entire state of New Mexico at that moment.

"I always turned good into chaos," I heard myself begin. "From the time I was old enough to make a mess, I did. Not you. Always sensible, always practical, always dependable. The only thing anyone could ever depend on me for was knowing if you gave me enough rope, I'd hang myself often from the highest tree."

"What's anything about, Dana? What's the point? How does any of this make sense?"

"That you, Missy?"

It was Sam's voice. I squinted until I could see him walking through the falling snow. When he reached the boulder, he literally floated to the top, like one of the snow flakes. I noticed he did not wear anything different than what he always wore. A long sleeve cowboy style shirt, ragged old jeans, and a dirty Stetson hat. He wouldn't be cold. I doubted he noticed the storm.

"Not Missy," I answered. "Myra."

"Hard to get used to Missy being gone," Sam said.

"Why didn't she return? Like you? You came back here the day they buried you."

"I always liked this place. My whole life. I first met Kopeki out here past the ruins when I was a real small boy. Played with Ben, too. Funny, ain't it?

Me and Ben was the same age, once. We ran all over these hills like a couple of little kids."

I turned to stare at him, sad at the idea so long ago. Sad that things change. People age. People die.

"You were a couple of little kids," I offered.

"Yeah," Sam sighed.

"I guess I thought she'd come back, too."

By now the snowfall slowed and the temperature dropped a few more degrees. I adjusted my down parka around my cold ears and snuggled deeper into the warmth of my clothes.

"Transition's a one-of-a-kind journey," Sam offered. "Nobody does it the same. Has everything t'do with how we wore our skin, ya know. Right minded idea you hear these days, the one about how big your footprints are, meanin' the ones you make and leave behind. Big footprints in kindness? Not talkin' about those. Big footprints all over the place. Them's the ones that'll mess up a good transition. Missy wore a real soft moccasin when it came to them big bad footprints. She wouldn't have to deal with such as that in her transition. But she did have one big loose end. Our Dana had a whole 'nother history that had nothing t'do with this place, or even with you. I know you were 'bout the only family she ever had. But you didn't even meet her till what, fifteen years ago?"

I nodded. Was that all it had been? I never even thought of my lonely empty life before I met my cousin.

Sam spoke again, "Missy ever tell you about her fella?"

I nodded and couldn't help but tense from the chill, noting his shirt sleeved attire, entirely inappropriate for subfreezing weather. My respiration seemed to crystalize with each out-breath. Sam appeared oblivious to my earth-bound sensations.

"Larry Tawayesva," Sam said. "Sheriff Zorro. She thought that fella hung the moon and set all them stars into the sky just for her." Sam shrugged. "Come to think of it, he thought that about her, too. He was killed, ya know. In the line of duty. That's the way Missy put it. Busted her up worse'n a broken heart. I bet her not being here with us might have somethin' to do with him. I bet he was right there for her when she crossed over. The two of 'em, they were a pair that shoulda had more time. They got time, now."

While we visited high up in the hills above the ruins, Mule wandered over from where ever he'd been hanging out, and now stood below us, leaning against our frozen boulder. I would have patted his big head, but I couldn't reach him without sliding off my frozen perch.

"Mule's a good ol' amigo, Missy." Sam was intent on now assigning Dana's nickname to me. I'd argued and protested half a dozen times during earlier weeks to deaf ears. Seated here with Sam on this frozen rock smack dab in the midst of a winter storm sharing thoughts, I now realized what reverence I'd been granted. Sam and all the others, including Mule, had no higher regard for anyone or anything than they had for Dana. For them to bestow her nickname upon me, well, I didn't deserve such esteem. From this moment forward, I would be Missy.

Lost in the seconds between my own notions, Sam made his exit. I'd failed to see him leave, and wished I'd thanked him for our conversation. What he said held water, and I would stop myself from wondering why my cousin had not returned. I'd cease the self pity and preoccupation with my grief. I needed to move on. I needed to find a life and learn how to live it without family, without alcohol. After all, I'd learned to navigate the day to day events of my life without my ex-husband. Of course, that'd been different.

"I'll be okay," I announced to Mule while sliding off the boulder and hoisting myself onto his snow covered back. "Let's go home, mi amigo."

While he plowed through the heavy snow drifts, Rudy appeared at his flanks and loped effortlessly.

CHAPTER FOUR

I strolled into the hotel lounge and allowed my eyes to run a quick sweep of the room. Mostly couples were seated in the cozy booths. I wasn't sure why I was here. To drink, maybe? Or talk myself into not drinking. Bailey was comfortable at home, and if I did drink, I wouldn't be able to drive. She'd need to go outside soon. Perhaps Ben would show up and let her outside. But, he probably wouldn't. After all, a person shouldn't count on their neighbors to be responsible for their own pets.

"Ready to order?" the young man asked. He appeared to be all of fourteen years old, hardly old enough to serve alcohol. Since I'd hit my forties, anyone who wasn't at least forty had begun to look about fourteen years old to me. Most of the team who'd cared for Dana had certainly failed to pass the over-fourteen test, too. I'd even asked one of the doctors his age. "Thirty-two," he'd answered. I never did believe him. He wasn't fourteen. I think he was twelve, give or take a week.

"Need a few more minutes?" the waiter inquired.

"Sure."

"Okay. Just wave when you're ready." He stopped at a nearby booth and began taking their orders. Before he headed for the kitchen I called him over.

"Grilled cheese on sourdough," I said. "And coffee."

"That all?"

"That'll do it," I said. He smiled and left. Probably thought I could have gotten that in a dozen cheaper restaurants. Probably wondered why I didn't order alcohol. I'd self-talked myself out of it. Reminded myself about

Bailey, and snow on the highway, and the need for a clear head. I hadn't had a drink in so many years that my efforts to self-talk myself into remaining sober had gotten easier. Still not simple. But less complicated.

While waiting for my equally simple dinner, I overheard the couple next to me arguing. I tried not to eavesdrop, but their voices carried the pitch of anger making their words impossible to ignore.

"Why'd you take that money?" the man asked.

"They always have so much," the woman replied.

"What do you mean?"

"Well, they do."

"That's what they do! They invest other people's money!"

"Yeah?" The woman giggled. "So when will they miss a few thousand."

"You're crazy!"

"Sometimes they actually have suitcases full of cash."

"But it's not yours." The man's tone turned from surprise to frustration. "You stole somebody else's money."

"You think?"

"What the hell, Veronica!"

"What should I do?"

"Give the money back."

"I spent most of it."

"What?"

"Well ... I did."

"What'd you spend that much cash on?"

"You know," she whined.

"No. Tell me."

"Clothes. Shoes."

"You can't spend that much cash on clothes and shoes. Veronica, you're screwed. If he doesn't kill you himself, he'll have you arrested."

"Arrested? You think I'd go to jail?"

"Damn, girl. If you can't give the money back, you'd better run."

"Where would I go?"

"I have no idea, but you'd better get out of Santa Fe. That's for sure."

"Grilled cheese and coffee," the waiter interrupted my eavesdropping.

"Thanks," I said.

"You need cream?"

I shook my head no.

"I'll refill your coffee in a few. Just put a new pot on."

"Thanks," I said. I wished he'd go so I could hear more. Too late. When my waiter left, so did the couple with the stolen money issue.

After eating I savored one last cup of brew before returning to the parking lot and discovering one of my tires appeared low. I drove slowly to one of those discount tire stores near the mall and had them check it. I'd picked up a nail. While waiting for the technician to repair the tire I worried about Bailey, reminding myself it didn't matter. Worry didn't change things. I'd be late. I looked at the positive side: I had a flat in the city instead of along a dark highway in a snow storm. When the repair was complete and the other three tires were checked over as well, I headed home along ice covered highways.

Bailey burst through the doorway soon as I unlocked it, bounding into the winter night to relieve herself and take in a bit of exercise. I took a hot soaking bath, made a cup of tea, found a Christmas movie, and was settling into my late evening when I heard Bailey going cracker-dog crazy in the distance. Her barking seemed much too far away and I immediately jumped off the chair and pulled on my snow boots and parka. Her frantic barking intensified, which was odd. This never happened before, and I feared for her safety. Perhaps a mountain lion, or a bear, was threatening Bailey. I was glad for the full moon which illuminated my way while I pushed through knee deep snow following her sharp shrill barks. I estimated I was within a few hundred yards of where Bailey's barking originated when suddenly the night turned into brilliant colors, like July the Fourth, and an enormous explosion blasted the winter sky. What followed was a parade of flames leaping high into the air.

"BAILEY!" I screamed as loud as I'd ever screamed.

"Woof! Woof! Woof!" She echoed back. I was at first so relieved she was safe that I didn't think about what had just happened.

"Here, girl! C'mon." I called out and she raced to meet me. "What in the world is going on? What did you find?" I dropped to my knees in the frozen snow and hugged her cold fur.

"Woof!" She broke loose and raced toward the shooting flames. I followed moving more cautiously. The snow was deep and there were numerous low areas covered in drift. If I stumbled into one of these, I would drop beneath the surface and freeze to death, if I didn't suffocate first.

Finally what felt like hours later but amounted realistically to a mere few minutes, I emerged on the scene of a car fire. Bailey raced back and forth, barking frantically at the blazing inferno of steel, plastic, rubber, and fabrics.

"Looks like someone stole it," I said out loud. "Probably decided to dump it. But how'd they get here? I'm a good mile off the main highway. This isn't anywhere near the road ... and there's a barbed wire fence. They must've drove through that."

It occurred to me that whoever set this vehicle on fire might still be around. But, that was not likely. Bailey would have gone straight to anyone who was stranded out here. I watched her, and her focus was upon the car.

"C'mon, Bailey. Let's go home. I need to phone the sheriff."

"Woof, woof, woof, woof!" She didn't intend to follow. I guessed the explosion and the burning tangle of what had recently been a vehicle was too much excitement. She could not calm herself down. I left and made my way to my house.

Once inside I continued to be cautious. After retrieving my handgun, I checked every room and closet, made sure no one found sanctuary here. I would always remember my run-ins with Haggis. I never trusted anything I couldn't see, after Haggis.

When all was clear, I phoned dispatch, described what I'd witnessed, gave directions, and waited at my house until a sheriff's deputy arrived.

"You Myra Whitehawk?" the deputy asked.

"I am. Someone torched a vehicle out on my property, about a half mile from here."

"I see the fire. Can we get there in the patrol car?"

I shook my head. "No."

"You see anyone? Any tracks?"

I shrugged. "Nothing."

"Somebody had to drive it out there. Right?"

"Yes. But there's no road out there. They would've driven it through a fence and probably bogged down in a drift. I have no idea why anyone would be way out here off the highway. Especially with this much snow. Makes no sense to me."

"Might be stolen," he said.

"I thought of that."

"Driver might still be here." The deputy's hand moved instinctively close to his side arm.

"I doubt it. Bailey would've alerted to a person hanging around."

"Bailey? Is that the dog I hear out there?"

"She discovered it. I guess you could say she's an eye witness, may have seen who did this. I heard her barking pretty crazy-like. She's getting more frantic. Makes me think she saw the whole thing."

"I'm gonna call for back up," the deputy said. "Driver might've headed out to the highway."

"Good idea," I said, remembering Haggis again.

"I'll get my flashlight," he added. I waited while he returned to his cruiser, called for back up, found his flashlight, then reappeared.

My mind tripped over gratefulness that I had decided not to get drunk this night. Haggis had butchered Rudy. Killed my young dog, but couldn't harm the Spirit Wolf that emerged from Rudy's puppy soul. That Spirit Wolf hunted Haggis down and ripped him apart. Haggis had bled to death in front of a couple of shocked Navajo policeman.

But Bailey wasn't a Spirit Wolf. If someone killed her, she'd be dead.

Damn! I was so relieved I'd talked myself out of drinking.

I took the lead and we made our way out to the site. Two additional deputies arrived around midnight and I left the three of them to their work. Bailey had grown bored with the situation, and we both hurried to the warmth of our beds. I slept sound until the phone woke me up around nine the next morning.

Chapter Five

"Are you Myra Whitehawk?" A man inquired.

I paused to glance at my caller ID. State Police. "That's me."

"You had a vehicle fire on your property last night."

"Sure did."

"Santa Fe County turned the case over to us. My name is Detective Shaw."

"Was it stolen?"

"No. Sheriff's report says you didn't see or hear anything until you heard your dog barking. That correct?"

"Correct." I was always cheap with words when I didn't know the game.

"We're sending the crime scene investigators out this morning. You going to be home?"

"Probably. Is the car still here?"

"It is." Detective Shaw paused, weighed how much he wanted to offer, and obviously decided to be stingy.

"Okay," I replied.

"We've got a deputy and a state trooper with the car."

"Okay."

"We'd like to ask you and your dog to stay clear of the area."

"Okay."

"I'll stop by your house later."

"Okay."

"Any questions?"

"No."

While brewing a pot of coffee and dropping wheat bread into the toaster, Ben showed up. He ignored me, more interested in observing the process of bread toasting. When the pieces popped up, he stepped back and grinned.

"You want a piece?" I asked, spreading peanut butter and honey across both slices.

He shook his head no and continued to grin.

"What's funny?" I asked, carrying coffee and toast to the counter and sliding onto one of the bar stools. Ben leaned on the counter across from me.

"I know why Bailey was upset," he said.

"Yeah," I said, "I know that one, too."

"But I know *why*." He emphasized the *why* part.

"Car fire."

"Maybe," he said. He was still grinning.

I settled back on the stool and placed my coffee on the counter. "Okay, Ben. You're so smart. Why was Bailey upset?"

By now Bailey had sidled up to Ben, who scratched the fur behind her ears. She leaned her head into his hand to encourage as much scratching as Ben was willing to proffer.

"Me and Bailey heard the bitch screaming."

"I'm sorry?" I tried to hide my shock. I'd never heard Ben use profanity.

Ben seemed proud of his witness status.

"You … saw?" My response was slowed by the bitch part.

"Me and Bailey, we were chasing the Haggis rabbit. I hit it with a stick."

"You hit what with a stick?"

"The Haggis rabbit."

"And?"

"A car crashed in and the fence broke. Broke it all up. I wanted you to know, we didn't break that fence. Me and Bailey. We were just chasing … "

"Of course you didn't break the fence," I interrupted him. "So what did you see?"

"A man got out of the car that broke your fence. He yelled *you bitch*' and he dragged the bitch out of the car. Then he slugged her in the face. She fell down in the snow. He dropped her inside the car."

"The trunk?"

"That's what I said," Ben argued.

"Okay. Proceed."

"When he shut the trunk, she started screaming. He poured some magic water on the car. The magic water turned into fire. Bailey tried to bite the man. Wow, Bailey can get mean."

"Good god!"

"I tried to open the trunk." Ben seemed suddenly sad.

"Good god!"

"I'm sorry," Ben apologized.

"I'm not mad. I know you couldn't open the trunk."

"I didn't know how."

"Trunks need keys. It's okay, Ben."

"The man ran away. I tried to follow, but he could run faster than the Haggis rabbit. Bailey was barking at the bitch not to worry. Bailey told her she'd bark real loud and you'd come and open the trunk."

"Ben, don't call her a bitch." It was all I could think to say. Good god. This was horrible.

"It was her name," Ben sounded hurt.

"No," I assured him, "that wasn't her name."

"What was her name?" he asked.

I shrugged and shook my head. "I have no idea."

I shoved the toast and coffee aside and buried my head in my hands. How could I share this information with anyone, much less the cops? I felt sick to my stomach. A woman burned to death less than half a mile from my house while I sipped tea and watched a Christmas show.

Ben sighed loudly to let me know he was bored with the situation, then he ran outside to find Bailey and Mule. He was an ancient, but he was still only a child. I watched him catch up with Bailey and Mule, and they traveled side by side, like a trio of playmates in search of adventure, up and over the furthest hill in the distance. I didn't worry they'd interfere with the investigation. Their direction of travel was toward the old ruins.

Tossing the uneaten toast and rinsing my coffee down the sink, I decided to wait for the detective. It was going to be fascinating seeing how long it took them to ferret out the information Ben witnessed. Would be so much easier if Dana were here. How would she handle this? Funny thing about Dana, she'd probably ignore the entire unfolding event. I could see her out in our ceramics studio today, mixing clay, throwing a few pots. What would she say? I believe she'd tell the detective to wipe his feet at the door. She'd offer him coffee in Kopeki's cup and patiently listen to his ramblings. Then she'd thank him for dropping by, and she'd ask who he intended to send to fix her fence.

Dana concerned herself with her business. She didn't meddle.

I meddled. Who was the woman? Who killed her? Why?

A few hours passed before Detective Shaw showed up. I heard his tires crunching along through the snow in my driveway, which gave me time to pull my sweater over my shoulders and go outside to greet him.

Unfortunately, the Haggis rabbit was running for its life (for the hundredth time) around the driveway while an owl made swoops, razor talons ready. I hoped the detective didn't notice.

"What the hell was that?" Shaw said, jumping from his car and watching the hideous Haggis rabbit race away.

"I'm sorry?" I used my innocent expression.

"That thing! It looked like … I don't know what the hell it was."

"I didn't see anything," I lied, pretending to doubt him.

"Really? Damn. Well … I haven't slept in 36 hours."

"Thirty-six hours? I'd be seeing things, too. Let's go inside. Freezing out here."

Detective Shaw surveyed my tidy attractive kitchen and den area. He chose to sit at the fancy dining room table I'd never used. I offered him coffee, which he quickly declined. "I don't use caffeine."

"That's got to be a first. A cop who doesn't do coffee."

"Didn't say I don't drink coffee. I just don't do caffeine. Makes me anxious."

"I've got decaf."

"That'd be good," he smiled.

Pouring out the anxiety coffee, I rinsed the pot and refilled it with anti-anxiety coffee. While it brewed, I pulled eggs from the refrigerator.

"You hungry?" I asked. I imagined he hadn't eaten for awhile.

"That's okay," he waved his hand.

Ignoring him I scrambled up a plate of eggs, tossed on a few pieces of fruit, then set them on the table. He began eating, without realizing he'd already turned the food down. This guy really was tired. He'd activated his automatic button, and was eating because he was hungry, not because he realized what he was doing. I wondered why they worked such long hours. Would be hard to concentrate without focus. Suddenly a scratching at the door got both our attentions. I opened it so Bailey could enter. She stood near the entry and shook snow off her fur, pattered over to sniff the guest's shoes, then trotted off toward the living room to have a nap. Mule's big head appeared at the bay window, which was very near the table where Shaw finished the eggs. When he glanced up Mule startled him with stares through the glass.

"Jeeze!" Shaw didn't expect our visitor.

"That's Mule," I said. "He does that."

"Does what? Spy?"

"Yes," I grinned. "He spies. That's what he does best."

Welcome to my world, I thought. Your life will never be the same. I poured Shaw a large cup of de-stressed brew, and took a seat across from him at the never-before-used new table.

"You've got a lovely home," he commented.

I nodded and smiled.

"You live out here in the wilderness alone?"

"No," I said. "I've got a few neighbors."

"Neighbors?"

I knew what he meant. Dispatch would've already provided him all the phone numbers and addresses of anyone living within a mile of the crime scene. Cops enjoyed asking questions where they already knew the answers. I didn't provide him anymore clues about my neighbors. But, then, in rural areas, most people considered anyone else who lived there to be a neighbor, even if they lived several miles away. I did have a few of those type neighbors, too.

"Your name seems familiar," he fished.

"Myra Whitehawk? Don't know why. I'm not famous."

"Whitehawk." He stretched out his thought.

"My cousin, Dana Whitehawk, was engaged to a sheriff's deputy. Larry Tawayesva."

"Yeah, yeah, yeah. That's it. Yeah. I met your cousin. Tragic what happened to Tawayesva. Met your cousin at his funeral. Did she move?"

"She died before Thanksgiving. Cancer."

"I'm sorry to hear that," he said. He actually did sound sorry.

Settling back, I became aware how comfortable these set chairs actually were. Not only had I never used the table, I'd never sat in the chairs. I also studied the detective. Probably sixty. I wondered if he still enjoyed his work. Not likely. If he resembled others who career in one occupation, by the time they reach sixty, they're merely logging hours toward Social Security.

"Dana was an impressive person." Shaw sighed and drifted for a moment. Probably the cancer thought. People always knew someone who'd had it and lost the fight.

I nodded. I didn't want to go teary eyed and sad. "How can I help you?" I asked.

"We've got more than a car fire. We haven't brought out this latest fact."

"What would that be?"

"Someone was in the car. Medical investigators took the body down to University of New Mexico. That's where they determine cause of death and ID the body."

"How horrible!" I faked my surprise. "That explains why we didn't find a driver wandering around." I threw the last part in.

"Wasn't the driver," he said.

"Oh?" My turn to fish.

"Body was in the trunk."

I gasped. Hearing it again made it more horrible.

Shaw continued. "We've got a homicide. Ugly business. Medical Investigator will tell us if it's a man or woman, and if they were alive when they burned. Ugly business."

I listened past the words Shaw offered. He should retire. He didn't have the stomach for this stuff anymore. I could tell it bothered him. Dana told me something Tawayesva once told her. He said *when the victim becomes a person, it's time to go.* Dana said that meant objectivity was out the window. Pure investigation required viewing the scene and the victims as objects with clues.

"Homicide," I said, realizing I'd shivered a bit. Must've slid my mind back to the days of Haggis. Those were truly scary times.

"We're a little worried about you."

"Me? Why?"

"Whoever did this will probably return to the scene. They usually do."

"Why?" This was an aspect I overlooked. The thought made me shiver more.

"They think maybe they left something. They start worrying about things tracing back."

"I'll be okay," I lied. What would Dana do? Shaw was correct. This was bad.

"Do you have somewhere else you can stay?"

"This is my home. Of course I don't have anywhere else to stay."

"You aren't a witness, and you aren't a threat to this person, yet. But if they return here, and you stumble on them, you're a witness."

"I've got guns," I offered quickly. I wasn't leaving my home.

"I'm guessing whoever did this has a few of those, too."

Detective Shaw lingered and tried to talk me into moving for a few weeks. When he drove away, Mule and I watched his taillights flicker while he navigated the snow drifts.

CHAPTER SIX

By evening the news was all over local channels, and turned up on a couple of the national networks. Crime scene investigators swooped in, collected the body and the car, and spirited everything away before I realized they'd left. I guessed the car and the body were at UNM. That's where the State's best forensic crime lab was located.

I pulled my shotgun from the closet, where I usually kept it locked away. I'd done that ever since Ben discovered it in my truck years earlier, fired a round, and set Dana into a fit. I carried both shotgun and hand gun into my den, lit a few logs in the fireplace, then sat on the floor and began cleaning them. Firearms were more dependable when they were cleaned, oiled and full of cartridges.

Twice I jumped up and ran around my house to recheck all the doors and windows, make sure everything was locked tight. I wished Rudy were here, or at least nearby, but he didn't function that way. The Spirit Wolf traveled along a continuum of time unlike anything mortals, or ancient ghosts, understood. I had never been able to call him. Nakani said Rudy was *always and never*. I wasn't sure what she meant, but I had agreed. When he showed up, or when he left, these moments were as unpredictable as they were unplanned.

After cleaning my firearms, I loaded them.

An artificial peace settled over the house, the type of calm we give ourselves when we believe we are safe. If I'd learned anything from Haggis, I learned there is no such zone.

My telephone rang a little after ten that evening.

"Yes?"

"Detective Shaw, here. Sorry to call so late. How are you?"

"Well armed." Probably not the reply he was used to getting.

"It looks like we've got the perpetrator."

"Really?" I must've sounded almost disappointed. How could it be that easy?

"The victim is a woman. Car was registered to her. We've pulled some prints in and around the car. They belong to her boyfriend."

"That's good ... I guess?"

"Might be a second person. We're assuming the perp was picked up by an accomplice."

"How likely is it you'll find out who that was?"

"We'll see if the perp will tell us."

"You think this accomplice will show up out here?"

"Hard to say," Shaw paused. "Might have been more involved than just helping with a ride, you know. If that's the case, they have good motive. They'll be worried about clues, too."

"It's snowing again," I offered. "Will make travel in this area difficult."

"It will," Shaw said. "But you never know how desperate a person might be."

"I'll be on the lookout. I've got your card. You'll be the first to know if I have any news on my end."

"Sorry to call so late," he apologized again. "By the way, Merry Christmas."

The phone line closed before I could return the greeting. Christmas? Already? I'd completely forgotten. I threw a few more logs into the fireplace, replaced the screen, curled up on the sofa, and fell asleep.

I awoke early Christmas morning. The fire was blazing and Bailey was missing. Obviously Ben's doings. It was still dark outside and second thing I noticed were lights on down the hall; they came from my living room. Kopeki and Sam? Unlikely, since they'd have coffee brewed and I'd hear my television blaring. I walked quietly toward the living room and peeked inside. A two foot tree -- not including the large pot it was planted in -- stood between the television and my rocking chair. It was fully decorated with delicate porcelain animals: a mule, a dog, a dove, chickens, a rooster, and one white wolf; and there were shiny gold and silver pine cones hanging from string.

"How beautiful," I gasped.

Beside the tree lay a large box wrapped in Dana's favorite Christmas foil. I stooped and picked it up, pulling off the foil to reveal an exquisite bowl. The porcelain clay it'd been fashioned from was Dana's private recipe: a combination of red and black, fired to mix the colors in swirls around the bowl's circumference. I turned it over.

"For Cuz. I'll always be near. Love you bushels. Dana."

When had Ben done this? Yesterday? Last week? I hadn't bothered to come into my living room, except when Sam and Kopeki were here the day Dana died. I slumped in the rocking chair, cradling the precious bowl, and lost myself in grief. The tears continued until my sinuses grew congested from crying. Reluctantly, I set the bowl on my coffee table and left to find a box of tissues.

Later, while sitting on the floor in front of the beautiful tree, I wondered why Kopeki and Sam hadn't told me about it. Why didn't Ben say something?

When Bailey and Ben returned with Mule a few hours later, I opened the front door and called out. "Ben! Can you come inside, please?"

Bailey and Mule disappeared off toward the ruins while I waited for Ben.

"I found the Christmas tree, and the gift from Dana. Thank you so much."

Ben stared at me with his big brown eyes.

"The tree? The gift?" I asked.

He continued to stare. He truly was confused.

"You knew about them?"

He shook his head.

"Did Nakani ... no, she'd never do something so thoughtful."

Ben shrugged his small frame and grinned. "Probably the magic White-Hawk," he said. He turned and ran out the door, hurrying to catch up with his playmates.

"Dana?" I heard my voice trail behind him.

It was a mystery. The decorations were all made by my cousin's hand.

And it was always Dana who brought in the tree. Never cut. Always alive like this one, carefully potted in a large container, to be planted after New Year's. And the porcelain bowl. It was the most exquisite piece of pottery I'd ever seen. She always kept her special pieces for gift occasions. I wondered when she'd made this. She must have worked on it at midnight to keep it such a secret.

I'd heard of times when people pre-ordered gifts, which were to be sent at later dates. The people then passed away, often due to unforeseen accidents, and when the gifts arrived it was as if they were sent from Heaven. This felt like one of those times. But I couldn't shake the feeling Dana had actually been here in recent days. Of course, wherever she was, I'm sure time did not matter and there were no days, weeks, years. Only moments.

What a wonderful moment.

My eyes teared up again and I let the grief erupt.

All Christmas day I remained indoors. My porch thermometer read ten degrees outside, the wind howled and I kept a flame in the fireplace.

The day after Christmas I busied myself loading the dishwasher while a local television news show played on the small flat screen in the den.

"New Mexico State Police are now saying the body discovered in a burned car in Santa Fe County a few days ago has been identified as that of Veronica North. North worked as a clerk in an investment broker's office near the capitol rotunda. Her coworkers reported last seeing her when she left, alone, on a lunch break the day she disappeared. A person of interest has been questioned, and is being held without bond on unrelated charges at the Detention Center in Santa Fe. The District Attorney's office will not comment further."

"Veronica?" Sounded so familiar. Why so familiar? I didn't know anyone with that name. I ran it through repeatedly until I made a connection. The couple arguing in the booth next to me at La Fonda the other night, he called her by her name. Veronica.

Could this be the same woman? I raised up from the dishwasher in time to catch a quick glimpse of their suspect. Well, that wasn't the same man. The fellow I'd seen was a white guy, and he had a clean shaven face. Their suspect was a thin hispanic with a mustache. Both were probably mid to late thirties.

I replayed the conversation several times in my mind, wishing I'd paid more attention. The man told Veronica to return money she'd stolen from someone. Who'd she take the money from? A family member? A friend? An employer? I couldn't remember. People steal money from each other all the time. I did not think his warnings were serious. I believed he exaggerated, wanted to scare her into doing the right thing, returning what she'd taken. They did not behave like a couple, and for that reason, I hadn't put them together that way. I wondered how all this information tied together. One thing I was fairly sure of, the man I'd seen at La Fonda did not kill Veronica North. I knew at some point the cops would make a connection, but he wasn't a killer.

My instincts were seldom correct.

This time my hunch was right on.

Maybe.

Of course, I'd been wrong before when I had a hunch.

Oh hell. I'd give him the benefit of the doubt.

Now for my questions about this pair.

Who?

What?

When?

Where?

Why?

My curious nose began to sniff.

Had to quit sniffing. The morning wore into noon and I really needed to check out that section of fence that the killer destroyed when he crashed it down. While I considered tools I'd need to make the repairs, my mind tripped over the obvious. Ben saw the killer. All I had to do was ask him to give me a detailed description. I'd see if it matched the man currently held for other charges but considered a person of interest. During my years working as a newspaper reporter, interviewing deputies, lawyers and D.A.'s, I learned that a person of interest meant zip zero nothing. If you were the person who found the body, you were a person of interest. If your phone number showed up on the victim's caller I.D., you were a person of interest. If you sold the person a hamburger an hour before they were killed, you were a person of interest.

Bailey and Mule showed up while I crammed tools into my large canvas bag. Already my fingers stiffened from the cold and I returned to my house to find my best thermal gloves. I'd misplaced them, and decided to borrow Dana's.

Why did I think borrow?

The thought made me sad.

I wondered how long, if ever, it would take me to think of Dana and all her stuff in the past tense.

Bailey and Mule trotted behind me through heavy snow to her adobe. They waited just outside her kitchen door while I rummaged through Dana's winter sweater chest and discovered she had not one but three pairs of new thermal gloves. I dropped two pair back into her sweater chest and slipped the third pair on. Already my hands warmed inside the gloves.

I'd walked almost a thirty yards when it occurred to me: Dana's house was comfortably warm. Not as warm as Dana used to keep it during winter, but tolerable.

Had I set her propane heater?

No. I was reasonably sure I had not. I shrugged. Dana set it. The day she packed her personal items, those few things she thought she'd need in hospice. It would be her nature to do that, knowing she'd never be back. Knowing she'd never need a cozy warm home again. She'd worry her plumbing would freeze. Dana seldom used the propane heater because she relied on her wood stove to heat the small adobe. I set a nice fire in the wood stove a dozen times since Dana passed, and for some reason I'd failed to notice the house temperature was fine without the burning wood.

Now, while I resumed my journey to repair the fence, I also knew one day I'd need to face what to do with my cousin's things. I wondered if I'd ever be there, emotionally. Probably not. But Dana wouldn't want her possessions abandoned. She'd want them put to use. Her clothes? She'd want someone to wear them. They fit me, but I couldn't bear the memories. I'd eventually box them all up and donate them to one of the charities in Santa Fe. Her house and furniture? Those I'd leave. I needed to visit the adobe now and again, and I would always want to see that little house as it had been during Dana's life. Right down to the colorful spread on her kitchen table.

Too much thinking. These thoughts caused me grief. I threw my left hand in front of my face to act as a stop sign. I told myself to quit. It worked. My mind trailed off to the chore ahead.

Luckily the fence posts were intact. Not one busted when the car careened through, which was surprising. I guessed the barbed wire pulled them up from the frozen ground. The wire, on the other hand, was busted in so many places, it would be easier to run strands. I had plenty of new wire. I cut the posts free, replanted them in the same holes they'd been extracted from, and ran three new strands of wire. I added stays for stability and finally surveyed my finished project before returning home to thaw out.

At some point shortly after I thawed enough to take a warm bath, I heard Bailey scratching on the kitchen door. She was alone. Mule had tired of their adventures and returned to wherever a ghost mule might return.

CHAPTER SEVEN

As I predicted, the cops made a connection. Veronica North's dinner partner, the man who argued with her to give the money back, was now their primary suspect.

Cory Dunlap. The television news anchor identified him on New Year's Eve. Dunlap was a bit of a transient, the anchor said. He drove cattle haulers, didn't have a steady address and was nowhere to be found.

"Maybe they killed him, too?" I directed my question to Bailey and she actually seemed to smile back at me.

"You know something you'd like to share?" I asked.

"Hhhhwhmm." Bailey had no further comment.

"Be that way," I said, turning my attention back to chopping vegetables.

"Corey Dunlap, cattle hauling truck driver, and Veronica North, clerk for an investment broker in Santa Fe." I began my solitaire discussion. Bailey snored from Kopeki's blanket in front of the fireplace.

"Why would Dunlap go missing? He is without a motive to murder. He is practically unrelated to the crime which was entirely committed by Veronica. Hardly seems serious enough to get killed over. What's the link?"

I'd coaxed the killer's description from Ben, and was absolutely certain, neither Dunlap nor the man currently in custody for other unrelated crimes, was guilty. Ben described a middle aged man with blond-white hair. Dunlap's hair was brown. The man in custody had black hair.

"Our killer," I continued, "is probably late forties, early fifties, might be blond, might be silver haired. He is clean shaven. He has an average build.

Not tall, not short. Not heavy, not thin. And, he is a total sociopath. Only kind of person who could burn another human being alive. He's also very fit. Ben said he was fast on his feet, in spite of deep heavy snow cover and snow drifts. Now, for some reason, this guy is not known to anyone."

"It is a very good day for a cup of coffee," Kopeki called from the doorway.

"Come in, come in," I greeted. Kopeki was followed by Sam. They made themselves at home, prepared a large pot of coffee, took my best coffee mugs from the cabinet, and waited for the carafe to fill. Once they'd poured their favorite hot liquid into their mugs, they took seats at my counter.

"You fixin' some lunch here, Missy?" Sam asked.

"I am," I replied. My plate was complete. Deviled eggs, lettuce, carrots, cherry tomatoes, olives, diced cheddar cheese, sliced avocado, and pinto beans. I drizzled olive oil and vinegar over the whole mess, grabbed a napkin and fork, and sat with them at the counter.

"That looks like Mule's lunch," Kopeki eyed my salad.

Ben had already filled Sam and Kopeki in with the details of our recent event, and they did not have much interest in it, which seemed strange. But, why would they concern themselves? They existed on a different plane in a place I could not imagine. Crimes and tragedies and vehicle fires and murders: Sam and Kopeki earned more peace than having to be part of such sad worldly affairs.

"You knew Ben found some kind of injured critter," Sam offered while pouring himself another mug of brew.

"No? What is it?" My curiosity peaked.

"Don't know." Sam shrugged. "He won't share."

"It's a live critter?" I asked.

"Only kind that have injuries," Sam winked and smiled.

How silly. Of course it was a live critter.

"He hasn't said one word to me," I said.

"Ben is the critter keeper." Kopeki's tone ended that topic.

I finished my salad and was rinsing my plate, dropping it into the dishwasher, when both my visitors thanked me and left. I watched through my window while they walked off toward the ruins.

Angels and ghosts.

They could walk on water.

Or across snow.

Without leaving tracks.

While gathering an arm load of wood from Dana's woodpile, I considered Ben's new project. Next time he stopped in I'd ask him what kind of animal he was caring for, and find out if I could help with its wounds.

This day was already scheduled. I'd made an appointment with myself to go through Dana's closets and box up all her clothes. Not that I wanted to, but I sensed she wanted me to do this. I could almost hear her reminding me how many warm coats, jackets, sweaters, and snow boots waited for new owners.

"And you are correct, my dear cousin. It's a cold winter. Plenty of women will be happy to have such wonderful protection from the freezing temperatures and ice-chilly winds."

First, I laid a large crackling fire which quickly changed the little adobe from somewhat comfy to downright cozy. Next, I set a large mug of water into the microwave for a minute, then dropped in one of Dana's favorite tea bags: apple cinnamon. And finally, I threw the closet doors open, pulled out all the dresser drawers, and propped up the sweater chest lid.

Time to work.

I gently slid each piece of apparel off its hanger and folded the items neatly, dropping them into one of the four large plastic storage boxes I'd brought over. When her closets were empty I turned my attention to the drawers and sweater chest.

Her sweater chest revealed a surprise. Larry Tawayesva's well worn jeans and western style shirts. I'd had my share of overnighters and recognized these were clothes Tawayesva had worn and left here, probably the day he was shot. These were Dana's mementos, all she'd had left of a man who put the moon and stars in the sky "Just for her," as Sam had said. Her aloneness and loneliness suddenly hit me like an avalanche. I never thought much about her life's disappointments, her losses, those things which must have caused her the same grief I felt on this day. With the gentleness she would have used when she handled these items, I replaced her cardigans over Tawayesva's things and shut the sweater chest. These were not mine to give away, and here they would remain. With new focus, I sent my attention back to packing.

Dana did not have that many clothes. She was practical and thrifty. However, the clothes she did own were all high quality and well cared for. What surprised and saddened me now was the fact everything was fresh and clean. In the days before she'd been admitted into the hospice hospital, she must have ran her washing machine and dryer day and night. I had to sit on her bed and cry. This caused me such grief I let my sadness swell and erupt until the day wore itself out and night blanketed the earth outside each window.

With my face badly swollen from prolonged intense weeping, I decided to leave the filled boxes at her house and fetch them with her old GMC truck the next morning. I'd drive to Santa Fe and deliver each box to a different charity. Dana wouldn't want me to drop everything at the first nearest charity.

"Do this right," I could almost hear her coaching. "You make sure as many people benefit as possible."

"I promise," I heard myself reply.

Bailey met me at Dana's kitchen door and together we walked slowly home. While walking I noted how lonely and cold my house appeared. I'd forgot to leave any lights on. But, I'd left early in the morning. There'd been no reason to turn lights on at that hour.

Entering my kitchen, I switched on all the lights for this side of my house and was surprised I could still smell strong coffee aromas left many hours ago by Kopeki and Sam. For the first time in my years living here, my heart pushed past capacity leaving me so overwhelmed with gratitude for Dana's neighbors, my neighbors, it was all I could do to keep from bawling like a baby, again. My face actually ached, and I talked myself into simply accepting that I was growing as fond of that peculiar assortment -- those unpredictable visitors who came and went from the ancient ruins -- as my cousin had always been.

The next morning I loaded the boxes and drove to Santa Fe where I delivered them to four different destinations.

While driving home a pair of owls took flight from an old cottonwood tree and passed just inches from my windshield. In a fractured second my eyes met with those belonging to the smaller bird.

I sensed its peace.

Serenity.

Tranquility.

Unmistakably otherworldly.

I knew Dana made her transition easily. I knew she was with Tawayesva.

Still, I missed her. Like oxygen gone from the atmosphere. I missed my cousin.

CHAPTER EIGHT

Almost a week had trespassed on my calendar before I completed my work in Dana's house. I boxed up her dishes, her odds and ends, her magazines and books, her wall art, her boots and shoes. One day I'd be able to let these things go, but not this day. Stacking them one on top of the other, I lined the back wall of her guest bedroom with each carefully labeled box. I also transferred all the food from her refrigerator, cupboards and pantry into my house.

These chores are a necessary form of suffering.

I'd rather jump from a plane without a parachute than do them again.

"I wish Dana were here," Ben said, running up behind me while I walked home.

"Me too," I agreed.

"You took all the food?"

"I did."

"Oh."

"And?" My curiosity peeked.

Ignoring me, as he so often did, Ben shrugged and ran off in the direction he'd arrived from. He did not head toward the ruins. He headed in the general direction of the hill where I'd released Dana's ashes into the wind. I decided Ben had pilfered food from Dana's house to feed his injured creature. I wondered why he didn't just ask me to help him. I'd help with whatever food he needed.

I picked up my speed and hurried home, changed to warmer clothes and hiking boots. Ben, of course, did not leave tracks in the snow, but I knew this terrain. I climbed the highest hill and began surveying the surrounding hills and valleys.

Just as I suspected. I could see Bailey and Mule loitering near a small cave like structure. That's where Ben cared for his patient. Carefully, I made my way across several hills and down a couple of steep slopes before I reached the cave opening. Soon as Bailey and Mule saw me, they trotted over to meet me and we walked together into the cave.

Ben had set up a very efficient camp as I imagined he learned many hundreds of years earlier. A pit was dug and lined with assorted smooth rocks gathered from dry stream beds. The fire was kept constant by the occasional tossing in of neatly bundled limbs and twigs which were compacted and bound together with long stems from nearby salt cedar and sage plants; and these bundles now stood four feet high, probably four feet deep, and stretched at least twenty feet back. Probably a month's worth of fuel. Behind the fire, covered in blankets taken from Dana's house, I observed the outline of Ben's new patient.

I stepped as quietly as possible toward the blankets, reached down and pulled them back.

"You must be Corey Dunlap," I said.

"You a cop?"

"You the one who crashed my fence?" I asked. I could have also asked, "Who torched Veronica," but I didn't because I knew he wasn't the perpetrator. Corey Dunlap's face glistened with sweat. I wondered where Ben had disappeared to while his patient lay here burning up with fever. "You're sick," I offered the obvious.

"Sorry about the fence," he said. "You know what happened?"

"No."

"The kid was there. He didn't tell you?"

"The kid's name is Ben. He kinda left this part out."

Dunlap tried to sit up, but couldn't manage. He fell back on Dana's blankets.

"You need a doctor," I said.

"Cops probably think I killed Ronnie," he said.

"Who torched the car?"

"Don't know his . . . name," Dunlap stumbled over uncontrolled coughing.

"How're you hurt?" I kneeled beside him and touched his forehead. Yeah. This guy was dying unless he got proper help.

"I'm shot," he said. The uncontrolled coughing resumed.

"Does Ronnie's killer think you're dead, too?"

"I think so."

"What happened?"

"Long story. Not sure . . . sorry." He began coughing and I quit the questions. His efforts to talk weren't helping.

"Think you could ride a mule?" I asked.

"That one?" Dunlap pointed toward the cave opening. I turned to see Mule spying on our conversation.

"That's the one," I said. "If you can manage to stay on his back, I can take you to my cousin's house. You can't remain here. You're gonna freeze if you don't die from your injury first."

"The kid's taking pretty good care of me here," he said.

"The kid can't change the weather. Cold front is moving in. Nights will reach zero."

"Your cousin won't call the cops?"

"No. She'd never do that."

"She won't mind?"

"She died in November."

Dunlap's turn to study me. He couldn't tell if I was serious or crazy. "How?" he asked.

"Cancer."

"That's bad. Sorry."

"Life's hard," I said. I motioned for Mule to enter the cave.

With a great deal of struggle and effort, I helped Dunlap onto Mule's back. I was impressed when he neither moaned or groaned, and I knew his pain had to be severe.

"Walk very slowly," I whispered into Mule's big ear. "We're going to Dana's."

Mule commenced his cautious trek toward home and I trailed behind in case Dunlap fell off and died before we got there. When we reached the yard, Ben flew up behind me on his swift little feet.

"You left out a few details," I said.

Ben grinned.

"Your patient is practically dead," I said.

"No," Ben protested. "He's just pushing out the bad spirits."

"Oh, really? I thought maybe he had a fever."

"No."

"Let's get him inside," I said. "You open the kitchen door."

Once inside, Ben helped Dunlap bathe in the bathroom. I made Dana's bed with fresh linen and the few blankets Ben hadn't taken to the cave. I turned up the automatic heater's core temperature, and waited for Dunlap, who emerged wearing only a towel. After Ben helped him into the bed, I had Ben show me the bullet wound. I was shocked.

"What did you do?" I asked Ben.

"I took the hard stuff out."

"The bullet," I said. "You dug the bullet out of his chest."

Ben grinned.

"The wound looks clean. You did a good job. Where's the bullet fragment?"

"Where I left it." Ben seemed extremely proud of himself.

"In the cave?"

"I'm tired," Dunlap interrupted. His eyes drooped heavy and he drifted into sleep before we left the house.

Once in the yard I turned to Ben. "No fires. Don't set any fires in Dana's fireplace."

Ben threw a questioning expression my way.

"We need to make sure the house continues to appear empty."

"Okay," he said. With that he raced off toward the old ruins.

While making my way across the field I began adding up the charges the cops could bring against me if they knew I gave sanctuary to a fugitive. When I ran out of fingers to count the crimes, I breathed deep and quit counting.

At home I was not surprise to discover Kopeki and Sam helped themselves to my coffee and were now in the living room watching sixty year old reruns of the "I Love Lucy" show. I stood in the doorway and caught one of the many scenes where Lucy has a lot of *splainin'* to do with Ricky. Kopeki and Sam exploded into fits of laughter. I shook my head and left. They'd seen those shows a hundred times. They always laughed as if it were the first. All of life should be so simple.

Ah, but they weren't experiencing life.

* * *

Nearly two weeks passed and to my disbelief, Dunlap's gunshot wound continued healing and his fever was gone. Ben knew some excellent ancient remedies. I didn't ask him what he'd done. He would only grin at me if I did.

I'd taken one day and driven all the way to Albuquerque, bought a few pairs of jeans and some fleece sweatshirts at the mall where I'd be one of hundreds of other shoppers purchasing men's clothing. Dunlap needed some things to wear, and I needed to not be seen getting them. His leather boots had an exterior oil which helped repel the snow moisture. I figured he'd have to use them if he ventured outdoors because I ran out of the cash he'd provided on the clothes.

The afternoon turned comfortably pleasant for this time in January.

Indian summer.

People always made the mistake of thinking Indian summer came in the autumn.

Not true.

I was an Indian.

Indian summer occurred in the winter. Usually in January or February when temperatures rose to unusually warm levels. My ancestors knew this was not good. Trees and plants would be tricked into thinking spring arrived and they'd often begin the process of throwing out buds. Within a few days winter always returned and the plants were sent back into their winter mode.

The buds died.

And the plant was none the better for the confusion.

"You need another blanket?" I asked Ben's patient.

Dunlap shook his head. I'd brought two yard chairs out from the ceramic studio and carefully placed them so that I could see any approaching vehicle, while no one would see Dunlap before I could hurry him into Dana's house. I did not have any jackets or coats which fit him, and although it was well into the high 50's this day, he needed the warmth of a blanket, which he wrapped himself inside while we sat enjoying the fresh air.

"One of these days I'll allow you the privilege of telling me what happened," I volunteered.

Dunlap studied me. He didn't trust me. Didn't matter. I did trust him. He was an okay sort of a person. He didn't talk much, and that wasn't because of his injury. He just didn't talk much. He appeared to have about as much curiosity about me as I had about him.

"Where does the kid live?" he finally spoke.

"Over that last hill. That'd be northeast from where we are sitting."

"I don't understand. Is there a house back there?"

"Why wouldn't there be?" I asked.

"No road. No light reflections at night. A long way from the highway."

"Yes," I agreed. "It's a long way from the highway."

"You always do that?" he asked.

"What."

"Answer with pure nonsense."

"Don't know," I said. "Don't usually answer myself."

He squared me with his eyes and did not say another word for a few minutes. I squared him back and sat with patience.

"You're very strange," he eventually said. "Don't mean that as an insult. Don't mean it as anything. Not sure why I bothered to say so."

"I've been called a lot worse by a lot better than you," I said.

We proceeded to sit without conversation for another hour, until the sun began its descent in the western sky. I wore my flannel insulated jacket, but could feel the cold inching through the cloth. "Brrrr," I said.

"Brrrr is right," Dunlap agreed.

We both stood. He started to pick his chair up when I carried mine to the ceramic studio.

"Leave it," I cautioned. "Might open that wound. Ben'd be disappointed."

"Ben and me, too," he smiled.

I kind of liked this Dunlap character. Or maybe I just enjoyed his company. Not sure. Didn't matter. I was going to help him get his strength back, and then, I don't know. Worry about the future? That's one worry that had never been big on my list.

CHAPTER NINE

According to what I'd heard on the news, and pulled up in court records via the internet, I discovered the police never made a connection to the mystery man who so brutally and degenerately murdered Ronnie North. By now I didn't think of her as Veronica because Dunlap never called her by that name. The night he argued with her at La Fonda, that night he addressed her as *Veronica*. When we are furious at another person, we often do that. A lot of people's parents do that. You disobey big time, instantly your name isn't Jane Doe. You are now Juanita Juliana Josephinia Doe. Or whatever.

Anyway, I understood.

Ronnie North was not Dunlap's girlfriend. They'd been neighbors in an apartment complex in Oklahoma City a few years back. But there'd never been a mutual attraction. When Dunlap's truck route brought him through the Santa Fe area, they'd hook up and have dinner if she didn't already have other plans. Ronnie had a boyfriend, and that guy was still behind bars on his unrelated charges. He was the cop's prime suspect until his alibi eliminated him.

February ticked away. Soon it would be springtime. Dunlap's gunshot wound was healing, he was okay, and continued hiding out at Dana's adobe. I'd begun to realize he didn't need to hide. No one returned to the crime scene. They were not particularly thorough since they'd missed blood in the snow. Of course, they'd not thought to look beneath all the snow which fell after Dunlap escaped through the blanket of darkness that night, wounded, undoubtedly leaving some blood. Made me absolutely understand why there were so many cold case files in New Mexico. The investigators wanted a perp and Dunlap fit the ticket.

I remembered how it upset Ben when he described being unable to open the trunk. What I hadn't known, because he didn't say, was that during the pandemonium which landed Ronnie locked inside a blazing vehicle, Dunlap fought with the mystery man, was shot by that man; and somewhere in the midst of disturbance, rescued in the middle of a New Mexico blizzard by an ancient little ghost who guided him to a cave.

And so, when I'd absolutely made up my mind about what I imagined happened, my little box of answers turned into crackers, fell on the floor, and crumbled into useless pieces. I had been unloading my dishwasher, keeping the television on in the background tuned to a local news program, when I heard Veronica North's name. Setting a handful of forks on the counter, I stared at the news.

Veronica North was a liar and an embezzler, according to the anchorwoman. North was suspected of making illegal withdrawals from some of her employer's client accounts. Hidden cameras and microphones were installed by a local private investigator in the offices where she worked, and the banks they used for their client accounts were made aware of the operation. North died not knowing she was in big trouble.

Dunlap believed her. I was a witness that night at La Fonda. She accused her employers of crimes, and pretty much told Dunlap she was lifting cash from cash lifters. Not according to this information, and I could be reasonably sure, since several large banks had been involved in catching her, the investment firm was on the up and up.

This left me with one problem to obsess about. The mystery man.

Who the hell was he, and why did he car jack North and Dunlap, brutally murder North, and attempt to murder Dunlap?

My thoughts tripped back to Haggis.

Mystery man was a psychopath.

I could take all this information to the cops.

They'd assume I needed strong medication.

Especially in the part which included Ben.

Okay, so I wouldn't take any of this to the cops.

Maybe I'd try to find this character.

After all, I found Haggis and Rudy killed Haggis.

Just then I spotted the Haggis rabbit racing across the yard outside my kitchen window. In seconds Bailey and Rudy followed, hot on his trail. If Dunlap saw this, it'd be difficult to explain. Anyway, far as I knew, Sam and Kopeki were having coffee with Dunlap. Dunlap introduced them to Clint Eastwood, and now every time I peeked in at coffee time, instead of cartoons and 60 year old *I Love Lucy* reruns, I'd hear *Hang 'em High, Dirty Harry, Play Misty For Me,* or one of the other Eastwood flicks. Kopeki had some new favorite phrases, too: *Make my day* and *Do you feel lucky, punk.*

After switching off the television, unloading the dishwasher, and admiring the exquisite bowl which graced my counter, the one Dana left me for Christmas, I made my way across the field. Might as well get this over. Not wanting to include Sam and Kopeki in problems of the living, I motioned for Dunlap to follow me outside.

"Veronica was embezzling money from her employer's clients."

Dunlap's expression revealed surprise and disbelief. "Why would you say that?"

"Heard it on the news."

"No, no. That place where she worked, they're just making that up to cover whatever they're up to."

"They hired a P.I. and involved several banks. They were about to have her arrested."

At that exact moment, the Haggis rabbit flew in front of us. Rudy loped easily on his heels and Bailey bounded behind Rudy.

"Good God!" Dunlap jumped.

"Strange, isn't it," I added.

"What the hell!? What is it?"

"It's deformed," I said.

"What d'ya mean?"

"It happens."

"Damn! Was that a wolf chasing it?"

"A few of those around these mountains."

Dunlap faced me with a dumbfounded expression.

"What," I shrugged. "So, it's a wolf."

"Will it hurt your dog?"

"They're the best of friends."

"Wow. I know I need glasses, but, wow. You don't even wanna know what that thing looks like."

"What does it look like?" I feigned curiosity.

"Creepy."

"You want some lunch?" I changed the topic. Bailey and Rudy grew bored with the Haggis rabbit, and both were long gone on some new adventure. Luckily, the Haggis rabbit was gone, as well.

We walked without talking toward my house. Once inside, I made a couple of cheese and tomato sandwiches and grilled them with butter. While we ate, I asked, "How well did you know Veronica North?"

"We were neighbors at an apartment complex in Oklahoma City. She tended toward the party stuff, so I never saw her as date material, if you know what I mean."

"No," I said. "Tell me."

"She has, I mean had, a cocaine problem. She liked to do all nighters with other party crowds. Not my idea of a life."

"But you were good enough friends to stay in touch and you visited her when your hauls brought you through Central New Mexico."

"I felt sorry for her. She was like the kid who always got what she wanted by acting bad. Tantrums. You know the kind. Kids who yell and scream and the parents give 'em whatever they want to make 'em shut up."

"I don't see how any of that makes a connection, but, okay. So she was a party animal who used too much nose candy, which meant she needed a lot more money than she ever had. You never wondered how she paid for her habits?"

Dunlap shook his head.

"She probably stole from all her employers."

"You said the place she worked wasn't doing anything illegal?"

"They were having her investigated," I said.

"So who was that guy?"

"Tell me again what happened that night." I did not tell him I was seated in the next booth and I heard their conversation. This inside information helped me observe how well he stayed with the actual facts. So far, he stayed with them.

Dunlap inhaled deeply, exhaling slowly. "We had dinner at La Fonda. Kind of expensive, but she insisted, said it was her treat. After dinner we were having coffee and dessert when she told me about the money. I can't remember exactly how she said she'd gotten it, but she blamed it on her employer, said they were doing something shady. Then she admitted she stole it and I told her to give it back. She said she'd spent most of it. My guess was most of it went up her nose, know what I mean?"

I nodded, "Continue."

"I parked my livestock hauler on the street in front of her apartment and we used her car that night. We left the hotel and were walking toward the parking lot when this man asked for a light. He had a cigarette in his hand. I don't smoke, but I had a book of matches in my pocket, so I reached for the matches and he pulled out a small handgun. Looked like a .22 and at first I thought it was a robbery. I reached for my wallet and he grabbed Ronnie. Ronnie tried to pull away, she told him he could have her purse and her rings. He twisted her wrist. When she started to scream, he slugged her in the face. I kept thinking somebody was gonna pull into the parking lot, or walk out of La Fonda, or off the street. The whole thing was kinda surreal, you know what I mean?"

I nodded. I did not add I was inside having dinner while this happened. "Go on."

"My mind was spinning with crap, telling me to go for his gun, or do something heroic."

I interrupted Dunlap. "I don't want to know what you were thinking. Just tell me exactly what happened."

"He started pulling her through the parking lot. She quit screaming because he hit her every time she opened her mouth. I think I jumped on him because we got in a fight. Didn't last long. He still had the gun. Told me he'd as soon shoot me in the head as put up with me. He motioned at Ronnie with the gun, asked which car. She pointed at her sedan."

Dunlap paused and looked at me, as if all this made any sense to me.

"Okay," I said, "then what."

"He grabbed Ronnie's purse and got the key, unlocked the car, made us both get in. He made me drive. Made Ronnie sit shotgun. He crawled in the back seat right behind me. Told me the gun was pointing at my back.

He told me to head out of town. Told me to pick a road without much traffic. I had no idea where we were going, but we ended up here. I figured we were both dead anyway, that's when I let the tires leave the highway and hit the snow. I had little control at that point and we tore through a fence and wrecked. I'd hit my head on something and was pretty confused. Next thing I knew, he was throwing Ronnie in the trunk and setting the car on fire and I tried to help her. He shot me. That's when I fell. Not sure what happened next. Then out of nowhere this little kid appears. It's freezing and snowing and he's not even wearing a coat. At first I thought, damn, so this is what an angel looks like. When the kid tried to get Ronnie out of the trunk, I realized he was just a little kid. The car was a ball of fire, and this little kid was trying to do the impossible. I don't know how he kept from getting third degree burns. He didn't even have a first degree burn. I guess I was too out of it. The fire must've seemed bigger, or something. But it was hopeless, and I couldn't stand up. All the while your dog was barking, running around, barking, it was crazy. I thought for sure somebody would show up. Thought there had to be a house nearby."

Either Dunlap had a story and he was sticking with it, or this was his story. A few small details changed between what he told me the first time and what he described now. That was normal. Our memories alter things as time passes. People who repeat the same identical story over and over, those stories are rehearsed, and not usually reliable. Ben's account of what happened was similar to Dunlaps, although there were gaps there, as well. More normalcy. No two people ever view the same event, and later recall it in the same way, not even ancient people.

"Cops think you did this," I said. "And if I didn't know about the mystery man, I'd probably think you were guilty, too. All the evidence keeps going back to you. I have Ben's story, which collaborates yours. Ben doesn't lie. He does omit things, but he doesn't alter them."

"Ben's my witness," Dunlap said. "His story will clear me so they can find the real killer."

"Probably not," I said.

"Probably not?"

"Ben's not going to be your witness."

"Why not?"

"Hard to explain. Trust me, he's not your witness. We've got to figure out who this creep is, where he came from, where he went."

"I'm a truck driver," Dunlap said. "And I'm not even a particularly smart one. You're talking investigation stuff that goes way beyond my pay grade. I can't help with this."

"Gotta be DNA, something, somewhere," I said. "Maybe on your clothes."

"What happened to those?"

"I've got them in a plastic bag," I said. "Your blood, maybe some of his blood. Maybe his hair got on your clothes. There will be forensic traces of that man on your clothes. You said you scuffled with him."

"I jumped on him and we wrestled a minute or two."

"That's all it takes. Saliva, blood, hair, fingerprint."

"Fingerprints? On my clothes?"

"You were wearing denim with a lot of brass buttons."

"I see where you're going. Yeah. Why don't we give the stuff to the cops and let them find the evidence, and maybe that will help them find him."

"You say there is a mystery man. They may not agree."

"Ben saw him."

"Ben's not a witness," I repeated myself. "Look, before we can get anyone to take your story seriously, we need some kind of proof this guy exists."

"What do we do?"

"I have some ideas," I said. "Go back to the adobe. Don't discuss this with Sam or Kopeki. I can do a lot of searching on my computer, but I may need to do some traveling around."

"How will you stay in touch? Phone service at the adobe isn't on. You got a cell phone?"

"Cell phones need a signal. We don't get coverage here. That means they don't work."

"What do you want me to do?"

"Nothing."

"You and your neighbors are good people," he said.

"They're a bunch of good old ancients," I said. "I'm doing this because it interests me. I'm not your friend, I'm not your family. But Ben thought you were worth helping, so I'm helping. As for the mystery man, that's the part where pure curiosity stirs my involvement."

"Thanks," he said.

Dunlap annoyed me with his simplicity and his lack of curiosity. Other than that, he was reasonably charming and easy going, and about ten years too young for my taste. I didn't want to see him sent to prison for something I knew he didn't do.

I spent much of the rest of that week on the internet scouring newspapers from coast to coast. I'd almost given up that line of research when I had a hit.

The Denver Post had a similar crime, but this woman was alone when she walked into the parking lot of a popular shopping mall. Security tapes showed her unlocking a car while being approached by a man wearing a hooded jacket. He seemed to be holding a cigarette, asking for a light, when suddenly he abducted the woman, using her own car to leave the mall.

The story ended up with the woman's charred body discovered in the truck of her burned vehicle, located on a seldom used forest road by a couple of deer hunters. The Denver police had nothing useful. Their images from the parking lot abduction showed a man whose size and height matched Ben's and Dunlap's description of the mystery man. Beyond that, he was cloaked beneath the hood of his jacket, and there were no witnesses.

This all occurred nearly one year earlier.

I'd been wasting my time. My searches were limited to the past year.

Mystery man wasn't striking that often.

I shook off my frustration and started all over. This time I searched newspapers, coast to coast, during the past decade. My efforts brought results. Approximately nine months before Denver, another woman was abducted. A waitress in her fifties, she worked in an all night coffee shop in Los Angeles. Her shift ended around midnight. A few days later she was found burned beyond recognition in the trunk of her own car on a lightly traveled road in the desert.

Ten months before Los Angeles, all the same circumstances, this time in Las Vegas. That woman was a stripper in her twenties. I kept up my searches until I had a pattern. Denver; Los Angeles; Seattle; Minneapolis.

Always happened in winter months. Always happened nine months to a year between incidents. Mystery man was a serial killer. His targets were random. He didn't know these women. With the exception of Santa Fe, all these locations had large international airports. With the exception of Santa Fe, all were shipping hubs. Maybe he didn't show up in Santa Fe. Albuquerque made more sense, and wasn't far from Santa Fe.

Did he work for the airlines?

Did he work in shipping?

Was he a salesman?

Or was he a transient who just happened to get an urge to burn women to death when he turned up in these cities?

He had no preference for types, either. The women ranged in ages from early twenties to late fifties. White, black, hispanic. With the exception of Santa Fe, all were alone, on their way to their cars. Something wasn't adding up. I needed to talk to Dunlap.

I barged in without knocking to find him vacuuming the adobe's old tile floors.

"I need you to tell me again how you and Ronnie left La Fonda together that night."

"Well, it happened like I said."

"No, I don't think so."

"You saying I'm lying?"

"That's what I'm saying."

Dunlap stood staring at me. At first he seemed defiant, then more like the deer in the proverbial headlights.

"We didn't leave together."

"Because?"

"She stopped to use the restroom before we left the hotel. When she came out, I could tell that look on her face. She was sniffing. I hate that stuff. I hate the way it makes people act."

"Cocaine."

"Yeah."

"So you told her what, you'd call a cab?"

"I told her I'd find a ride out to get my truck. She was already flying. Laughing. Acting hyper. I hate that stuff."

"I got that. You have bad memories of users?"

"My dad was an alcoholic. I hated him."

I nodded. I imagined a lot of people from my past hated me, too. I didn't mention I was an alcoholic, as well. "Why don't we go back to the place where she is leaving La Fonda alone?"

"She got pissed off. Told me she'd always thought I was uptight. That made me mad. Then she left. I got to thinking about finding a ride out to my truck at that hour, and decided I'd ride with her. By the time I reached her, that guy was already bumming a light for his cigarette. I walked up behind him and everything kind of started going fast motion."

"You lie to me one more time and I'm calling the cops."

"I won't."

"You better not."

"Didn't seem that important. I mean, I didn't actually walk out with her, but I did try to catch up. I was too late. I think if I hadn't been so uptight, like she said, Ronnie would still be alive. I can't stop thinking if only ... "

"Let it go," I interrupted. "You didn't kill her."

CHAPTER TEN

Veronica North's embezzlement habits clouded her own murder. To the local cops this was just another case of money theft, greed and murder. Except it wasn't. Dunlap had no knowledge of North's bad habits, other than the nose candy habit. He believed her story about the investment firm laundering other people's money, or whatever the story had been. And he still told her to give the money back. His sense of guilt got in the way of his originally telling me the whole story about their tiff in the hotel lobby, and her exiting alone. Their argument probably cost North her life.

Stuff happens.

All that old coulda-shoulda-woulda stuff.

If worry won't change it, don't worry about it.

Dunlap bungled our psychopath's plans while bad weather altered the outcome. Snow packed full tilt that night and the mystery man had no inkling Dunlap headed full throttle into a winter storm. Of course, without the storm two people would've been killed.

Serial killers pick targets based more on opportunity than criteria. According to Ben's details, this man was neither tall nor short. He was average. He was neither heavy nor slim. He was average. Not particularly muscular, yet capable of enormous strength. I guessed he worked out regularly in a gym, or he had exercise equipment at home. His thick hair was short, and I guessed, sported a high dollar cut. Blondish white in color. Not sure what his style would be called. I knew stylists used products which lifted hair into stiff straight shafts creating a short spiky finish, and that fit both Ben and Dunlap's description. He had sharp angles to his face: square jaw, square forehead, poorly defined cheekbones, long narrow nose, and no facial hair. According to Dunlap the man could be anywhere between forty and fifty. Dunlap said he wore earrings. Small silver dots in both ears. Odd, but hey, so were serial killers.

Damn. We were working with the physical characteristics of a few million men.

This would not be easy.

But Haggis wasn't easy, either.

Something I knew about Haggis, and something I knew about this character, they both had tells. Something they were obsessed about. Something unique to them.

I could find him.

Biggest question now was, where should I get busy looking?

Donning my warmest parka, sliding my hands into thermal gloves, and pulling on flannel lined jeans and sheepskin lined boots, I set out to find Mule. Didn't take long. He was standing with his big head pressed up against the adobe's single living room window, spying on Dunlap.

"Hey!" I called out. He lifted his head and looked my way.

"Want to go find a trail?" I yelled.

Mule loved to look for trails. This trait, I was certain, had to do with his job while a live mule. According to Dana, Mule was a rental ride. People could rent him for a day, or a week, and set out on their big adventures packing across rough terrain, up mountains, across valleys, or to historic places such as Acoma. The type people who rented horses and mules were usually lost within hours of setting out on their adventure. When this happened, Mule was trained to simply go back to the original trail and take them safely to their campsite.

"How did he know they were lost?" I recalled asking Dana.

"How would he not know?" she replied.

"Okay," I'd said. I did not know, at that time, what she meant. I did know now. Once a few years earlier, I'd taken Mule and gone in search of an ancient sacred place I'd read about. Five hours later we ended up back at the monument parking lot where we began our journey. I hated to admit, I'd been lost as soon as we ventured an hour from the monument. Mule knew

I was lost, so he climbed around the mountain until he grew bored, later found our trail, and hauled me back to the parking lot.

This day I wanted to be lost, high in the mountains above the world. Although a heavy snow pack remained across much of the area, Mule wasn't affected by temperatures. I could dress warmly, and the sun spread a wide canopy of rays from east to west and north to south, so I'd be fine. And when we'd traveled far enough, Mule would bring me home before sundown.

It'd been a very long time since I'd felt so refreshed and brand new. Whether due to the high country wilderness with no signs of human contamination anywhere, or the peaceful company of my friend and transportation, all went well. Later, just when daylight planned its exit and I could already see the moon, we reappeared in my yard. I stored away my saddle and tack, and rewarded Mule with two large cans of his molasses sweet treat, before retiring to my warm house, soaking in a hot bath, and settling down with Bailey in front of a crackling fire and the evening news.

"For the second time in less than two months, New Mexico residents are left wondering why someone is kidnapping women, trapping them in the trunks of their own cars, and setting those cars on fire, burning their victims. The newest victim was discovered by State Highway workers when they spotted smoke coming from a seldom used road in the southeastern most section of that county."

I could not believe my ears. Mystery man had struck again. I listened carefully so as not to miss any aspect of this second killing. My first thought was he'd blown his anonymity. Surely local and federal cops would make connections to the other similar murders and flush this guy out to be the serial killer I knew he was.

My second thought wasn't so much mistrust, as it was, well, lack of trust. I pulled my parka over my pajamas, grabbed a flashlight, then ran to my carport where I kept Dana's old truck parked alongside my car. Snow cover confirmed neither vehicle had traveled anywhere since I last used them days earlier. Dunlap hadn't been a suspect, as far as I was concerned, but the smallest thread of doubt could now be eliminated.

Now I had to get down to pure facts. Mystery man struck approximately once per year during the past decade. Why strike again so soon? What was it I didn't know? Could it have to do with Dunlap's messing up this creep's plan? What happened to these women before he killed them? Obviously, that was part of his ritual, and he didn't have ritual completion with Veronica North. This presented a new question. Did the cops have any idea as to what that ritual might be?

"No." I answered myself. Because the cops had yet to pull all these murders in and see the similarities, see the thumbprint of a serial killer. Best I could surmise reading all the newspaper articles for all the murders was that each event became isolated. Each town believed they had homicide by a known person. They weren't even bothering to cast a wider net.

A thought hit me. Why was I so dense? Probably the best reason this mystery man continued to hang around had more to do with Dunlap. Local news suggested Dunlap made it out alive. A serial killer who'd yet to be labeled such now had an eye witness who could identify him. When and if that happened, bingo, domino effect, all trails would lead to him. Motels, hotels, gas receipts, employer, travel, family. A serial killer's anonymity blown, his face visible in all media forms across the country. His family would find out what a monster he was.

Mystery man had to find Dunlap.

I wondered if he'd return to the scene. Probably. The serial killer knew Dunlap could not survive without help. The cops believed Dunlap skipped town, left the state. Serial killer wasn't convinced.

Could be the most recent killing had more to do with his worry and anxiety regarding Dunlap's knowledge than it did with ramping up his hobby. He might trip up, leave clues, attract attention. Until now he'd operated without scrutiny because no one suspected a serial crime. Maybe he'd already slipped up. Hopefully the cops would make a connection and Santa Fe and Valencia Counties would jump aboard with the State investigators, and combine interests.

I had a concealed weapon permit, which was good, because in the years since Haggis, I always carried a concealed weapon. Hell, I often carried an observable weapon. Didn't really make me feel safe, but it was leverage in my mind.

I nearly jumped out of my skin when the telephone rang.

"I'm trying to get hold of Myra Whitehawk."

"Speaking," I said.

"Detective Shaw here."

"Guess who I'm thinking about," I replied.

"That's why I'm calling. You heard about the copycat murder happened down in Valencia County?"

"What do you mean, copycat?"

"Looks like the victim had some enemies. She'd turned in half her family for manufacturing methamphetamines. VC sheriff's department said they've already taken two of her brother-in-laws into custody. Her parents said they believe that's who killed her. I'm inclined to go with this. I knew you'd be nervous when you heard about it, but we're convinced we've got the perps. They wanted it to look like the homicide on your property a few months ago. Wanted to assure you, there's no connection."

"How can you be sure?"

"The vic's parents were present when the two brother-in-laws told our vic she was going to burn."

"Burn has a lot of connotations," I argued. "You burn someone, you ruin their life. Doesn't have to mean you're gonna physically burn them to death."

"Are you worried we're wrong?"

"I am," I said. "I'd like to discuss some ideas I have about this with you."

"Sure," Shaw said. "You wanna come down to Albuquerque? I'll buy you lunch. How about tomorrow."

"Tomorrow is good. Where?"

"Applebee's, corner of Yale and Gibson, near the airport. Eleven beats the lunch crowd."

"See you then," I said.

I knew that he knew I'd spent my share of years covering crimes for central New Mexico small town papers. I also knew he was up to date on the Haggis stuff. An old cop like Shaw would've run full background on me before he ever met me. That's the way they work. Try to come up with answers before they ask questions. My background eliminated me from having any knowledge or connection with Veronica North, or her killer. But Shaw also knew, based on the Haggis connection and my personal flaws, that I had a tendency to get obsessed with the investigation. And he knew I was good at digging up bones.

How much of this would I share with Dunlap?

How about none.

Local news would let him know our mystery man was back.

Dunlap was a bit of a *compos mentis* sort of guy. Well over a hundred years ago Dunlap would've been one of those cowboys who drove a stagecoach across mountains and deserts and never complained. I could as easily see him turning hot steel on a forge fabricating horse shoes, or following a plow keeping crop rows straight. He was a good person. But he lacked flaws, and to find a serial killer one needed flaws.

What type of flaws?

Poor judgment.

Common sense out the window.

Holes in ones logic.

And, of course, unreasonable faith in ones own flaws.

I fit the bill. I was as flawed as they came without being too damaged to function. Unless I got drunk, then I was definitely too damaged to function. I hadn't had a drink in years and did not plan on one any time soon.

Tomorrow I'd let Shaw buy me a cheeseburger and fries, and I'd suggest he think about the possibility of psychopaths in the Land of Enchantment.

CHAPTER ELEVEN

Applebee's didn't even open until eleven, but since that's when Shaw wanted to meet, I figured he'd be there at least fifteen minutes ahead of time. Sure enough, when I drove by at 10:45, he already picked his parking spot and was standing in the empty lot leaning against a government issue generic sedan, chatting on his cell phone.

Never understood why cops had to always act like cops.

At five minutes past eleven, I headed back to Applebee's and pulled in, parked alongside Shaw's sedan, and met him in the lobby. We appeared to be their first customers so they sat us at a booth facing the boulevard.

We ordered and made small talk, Shaw answered his phone a couple times, and we waited for our lunch. The tables filled up quickly and a steady hum of people's voices settled over the place until it sounded like a bee hive. When Shaw finally spoke, he quizzed me about seeing anyone out on my property.

"The killer either has, or will, return to the scene," he said.

"Maybe. I haven't noticed anything."

"You wouldn't tell us if you had," Shaw said.

I smiled. "Why would you think that?"

"You wouldn't," he said.

"Probably not. Unless I had to shoot him."

"What are these ideas you said you had?" Shaw couldn't hide his interest.

"You entertain the idea you're dealing with a serial killer?" I asked.

"It is a possibility."

"There's a pattern."

"Valencia County was a copy cat case."

"I don't think so."

Shaw stuffed his mouth with turkey sandwich and watched me, waiting for more.

"I'm not giving this to you. I spent days reading newspapers from all across this country, going back ten years. Approximately once a year a woman is burned beyond recognition in the trunk of her car. Crime locations are always hub cities. Places with international airports and popular convention sites. Lot's of reasons a person might be in these cities, especially if only once a year."

"I'm interested. What cities?"

"You do your homework. I already did mine."

"You working this up for a newspaper?" he asked.

"Could be."

"Not sure what you're thinking but I can guarandamntee you it's not a good idea."

"People's mothers, sisters, daughters, they are going to be burned to death until someone makes this connection."

"I'll look into it, and if I see a pattern, I'll call in the feds. Tell you what, any stuff I can share with media, I'll call you first. But you gotta promise you'll leave this to us."

Our waitress showed up and refilled our decaf mugs. I'd accomplished what I wanted. Shaw would find out what I already knew. Dunlap didn't kill North, and the Valencia County woman's brothers-in-law didn't kill her. Hopefully Shaw and the feds would soon be on the trail of a man who fit the description Ben and Dunlap provided. Of course, they'd have to ferret out that description.

After our meal we walked out to our vehicles. Shaw's phone rang and I used the opportunity to exit without any further lectures from the detective.

Instead of heading home, I followed Gibson to the I-25 freeway, aiming for the badlands of Valencia County. I wouldn't be able to visit the VC crime scene, but I'd get some information about something. Wasn't sure what, but the information was waiting. I just had to find out who, what and where.

* * *

"Hi," I smiled at the convenience store clerk, one of those young men with a bad complexion who looked twelve. "My boyfriend borrowed my car last week. He hasn't returned it. He lives around here somewhere. I'm trying to find out where so I can get my car back."

"Tell the fuzz he stole your car."

"Don't really wanna do that," I said. "I've got a sketch and a description of him." I handed the kid a copy.

"Creepy guy. Haven't seen him."

"If I leave this here, would you ask the other clerks to give me a call if they've seen him."

"That your phone number?" The kid was reading my sketch copy.

"Yes. I'd really appreciate it. I'd like to get my car back."

"Why'd you loan your car to some creep you obviously don't even know that well?"

"Trying to help him get a job, know what I mean? He needed a car."

The kid shrugged. "I'll leave this here by the register."

"Thanks," I said.

My routine had a method. I left the freeway with each exit into Valencia County, and drove the entire length of each road which exited, until I ran out of towns. I stopped at every convenience store on those routes and left the sketch along with my story. I didn't start home until dark.

Poor Bailey. She was outside today. She'd be freezing her foot pads off in the snow by now, and I owed her a huge dinner. Stopping at one of the grocery stores in VC before hitting the freeway, I ran back to the pet food aisle and bought Bailey's favorite canned dog food. The cashier was cheerfully talkative, there weren't any customers behind me, so I shared my story, handed her money for the dog food, and a sketch of the mystery man.

"I remember him," she said, popping her gum between her teeth.

"You're kidding." I almost didn't believe her.

"Hon, he is truly an odd man. You can do so much better."

"When? Do you remember which day?"

"He comes in here every couple of days," she said.

"You're kidding!"

"If I were you, I'd just call a policeman and charge him with car theft."

"What time of day does he show up?"

"That's one of the reasons I remember him. We stay open all night, you know. I work the three to eleven shift. He's been showing up the past few weeks, always here around eleven. He was hanging around out in the parking lot night before last. My husband was late picking me up and your boyfriend tried to hit on me. I came back in the store and waited until I could see my husband's truck. Hon, he's not worth your time and I hope you get your car back."

Night before last. The VC woman was killed the night before last. I thanked the cashier, took Bailey's dinner, and walked outside the store. Glancing up I saw security cameras aimed in every direction. The cameras weren't static, they roamed, didn't miss a thing.

Mystery man was on camera. And so was his victim, I guessed. She must've been in this store that night. I couldn't call Shaw because I couldn't easily explain why I knew what this man looked like. I worried how to get this information to Shaw.

The cashier saved her own life by returning to the store to wait for her husband. Thinking about all this made me shiver. I ran to my car and switched on the heater. My whole body trembled, and not because it was cold. I took the extra time to retrace my route, stop at every convenience store again, retrieve my sketches, and let the store clerks know I'd found my car. No need directing attention at myself now that I had what I wanted.

While driving home later I had to wonder. Was the killer living in VC, or was he only here until he found his latest victim?

I didn't drive into my carport until nearly midnight. Bailey was furious. Dana's adobe was dark, no lights on. Dunlap used the bedroom on the other side of the house and he would not see my headlights, wouldn't know how late I'd arrived home.

I set a nice warm fire in the den, fed Bailey, fetched a blanket and pillow, and settled down for the night on my den sofa. I thought long and hard how to let Shaw know where to find the killer kidnapping his most recent vic.

Early the next morning I dressed quickly and put Bailey in Dana's old truck.

"We're going for supplies," I told her. Actually, we didn't need supplies, but that's what I wanted Dunlap to think when he saw me leave. I drove straight to the Santa Fe main library. There were numerous typewriters and word processors there which I could use anonymously. I borrowed paper from a librarian and clicked off a message, short and easy for Shaw:

The woman who was burned in her car might be on a security tape made that night at the all night market on US 6 near I-25. She wasn't alone.

Those tapes weren't kept indefinitely, but I hoped they'd still have a copy of that evening. I did not know how else to make this information known. After dropping the note into an anonymous envelope, I mailed it from a postal box downtown and returned home.

I spent that day in the ceramic studio mixing clay and showing Dunlap how to turn a pot on Dana's pottery wheel. Nakani showed up as we were wrapping things up at sundown.

"This clay needs more sand," she said, clicking her tongue.

"Don't touch it," I warned.

"Why does it need more sand?" Dunlap asked.

"Too wet," she said.

"No it isn't," I snapped.

"This is taking too long to dry in the pit," she said.

"It's not in the pit," I said.

"It will crack." She seemed determined to start an argument.

"No it won't."

"I don't want my bowl to crack," Dunlap protested. "I spent hours making this."

"If it cracks, you can make a new one," I said.

"You are mixing clay how long?" Nakani asked me.

"A few years."

"I am making clay for a very long time," Nakani said.

"Go home," I told her.

"I am home."

"Then I'll go home," I said. "Turn the heater down in here when you close up," I said to Dunlap. While walking home, Mule and Bailey accompanied me. I walked around to the sweet treat bin and give Mule several handfuls of his molasses oats. He walked back to the kitchen entrance with me, and watched through the window while I warmed a bowl of my homemade green chili. Bailey flopped in the den on her blanket and commenced to snoring almost immediately. We'd all settled in for the evening when a news bulletin began showing the security record from that fateful night.

How'd he get my letter so quickly? I guessed Santa Fe mail went from the postal box, into the main post office, and then right back out to local addresses the same day. Shaw didn't waste any time getting those camera records, and he didn't hesitate a moment putting this new information out to the public.

I watched mesmerized. Black and white footage revealed what I suspected. The mystery man, wearing what appeared to be a hooded sweatshirt and gloves, stood at the edge of the sidewalk in front of the store. A woman with short curly dark hair exited the store carrying a single sack. He approached her with a cigarette. She pulled out a lighter. They walked off together into the parking lot, seemingly engaged in a friendly conversation. Some distance away from the store she walked behind a large truck which was parked between the camera angle and her car. The security tape showed her car leaving the parking lot.

What happened? My guess is the mystery man disabled her in some way and took her keys, then left the parking lot transporting his victim in her own car.

Within minutes there was a rapid hard knocking at my door. I swung it open and Dunlap flew in.

"That should clear me!"

"You'd hope so," I said.

"You saw his face, right?"

I nodded. "You've got a good twenty pounds on him, and you're a few inches taller. Most important thing is you don't wear earrings. You saw a light from somewhere threw a reflection off one of his earrings?"

"I missed that. Wow, this clears me."

"Clears you from the VC crime," I said. "Not sure it clears you of North."

"But you said yourself, he's a serial killer."

"That is one thing I am convinced of, but it doesn't clear you. Okay?"

"What now?" Dunlap's excitement dwindled.

"We wait, I guess." At that moment, I really didn't know what was next. "You want a piece of cake?" I offered.

"Yeah," he cheered a bit. "I haven't had a piece of cake in months. Maybe years."

"Don't get too excited. This is the kind which comes in a box from the grocery freezer."

"I like those kind."

"You are one easy person to keep happy," I said, pulling dessert plates from the cupboard. Luckily the date on the cake showed fresh, meaning moist. I added a large ladle of blackberries alongside each slice, poured hot water over tea bags, placed everything on a serving platter and carried it to the coffee table in my den.

"I never had such nice stuff as you've shared with me," he said.

"I haven't shared anything. You give me money, I buy you some food and clothes."

"Ben saved my life, and you've let me live in your cousin's house. I'd have died that night if the kid hadn't helped me. And I'd be in jail right now if you didn't give me a place to live."

"I gave you a place to hide until the cops get this mess figured out."

"How'd you know I was innocent?"

"I was thinking about getting drunk that night. I was sitting a few feet from you and North at La Fonda. I heard you trying to get her to do the right thing. She wasn't having any of that. Your friend had a long history of similar problems, stealing from employers."

"Shows how much we don't know about people we think we know."

"That's life."

"This is real good cake," he said, finishing off his last bite.

"Plenty more."

"You don't mind?"

"Only if you make me get it."

Dunlap carried his plate to the counter beside the refrigerator and sliced off a second helping. "You want another piece?" he asked.

"No, thanks."

He returned to his chair. "Don't know how I'll ever repay you and your neighbors for all you've done."

"No need. Look, I knew you weren't guilty because I heard your last conversation with her. Cops wanted cuffs on somebody. You were it."

"That's wild! Why didn't you tell me before, about being there, at the hotel?"

"Sometimes less is more."

"Not like I get to call any shots. Woulda made me feel better, knowing you knew I was innocent."

"Things like that break down into *he said, she said, they said.* Take that to a jury, chances are high they won't buy it."

"Why not?"

"It's their nature. Best liars in the world can be found in a courtroom."

"What're my options?" Dunlap asked, his expression grim.

"Investigators are reasonably sure they've got the VC woman's kidnapper on camera. He wasn't a relative, like they thought..." My telephone rang before I completed my thought.

"Myra Whitehawk?"

"Detective Shaw?"

"Yes," he said. "I've got some interesting information. Promised I'd give it to you before it hits the airways."

"I'm listening."

"You were right. We've got what looks like unmistakable evidence connecting the two homicides."

"Not surprised."

"Cigarettes," he ignored my sarcasm. "I found an unlit cigarette in the parking lot where we think Veronica North left from that night. It's been bagged in evidence. One of the Valencia crew found another one, same brand, again unlit, in the last area the second woman was kidnapped. We've sent both to the forensic labs in Denver. They've got better equipment."

"Same man," I said. "I don't need forensics. He's a serial killer. You going to contact cold case investigators for all those old similars I told you about?"

"Already on it."

"Good."

"Thanks," he said.

"For what?"

"For your persistence. We pulled in the feds after talking with cold case colleagues in six cities with similar homicides. Like you said, all happened about a year apart."

"You going to filter Los Lunas area, in case he's still there?" I asked.

"Already on it."

"Thanks."

He didn't respond, he knew what I meant. The sooner they caught this guy the sooner my life shifted back to cruise.

"Be careful out there." Shaw sounded sincere. "We're going to patrol the highway which runs past your place every night. We believe he'll be back to review both of his crime scenes. New problem is why'd he hit twice in less than three months. It's a first for him, and there'll be a reason. You've got my card and my cell phone. You call if you even think something's not right. Oh, and one more thing. Still no sign of Veronica North's date that night. Looks like our perp got rid of him. You may find Corey Dunlap before we do."

"Meaning?"

"Lot of wilderness covered in deep snow up there. We can't afford the search and discovery necessary. Like I said, you got my cell. You call me anytime."

Shaw hung up and before I felt a need to reply.

"What's going on?"

"Mystery man left cigarettes at both abduction sites."

"You gotta be kidding!"

I shook my head and smiled.

"This is great!"

"Except for the part where he's still out there somewhere. And I think he's hanging around New Mexico till he figures out what became of you.

You're the eye witness. You're the only one who can positively say he is the killer."

"Not good."

"And," I paused, "investigators think the mystery man killed you, dumped you over there in the snow." I pointed toward the burn site.

"You're right. He has no way of knowing I'm not buried in a coupla feet of snow up there in one of them drifts. I need a gun, Myra."

"I've got an extra rifle," I said, going to fetch it.

"Double barrel shotgun," Dunlap seemed relieved when I handed it to him.

"Here's a full box of shells. You familiar with these? You better be. You've got one shot, and if that's not effective, you'll have to reload in a second."

"I'm good with shotguns," he said. "I was afraid you'd bring in a hand-gun. Never used a handgun. But I grew up using shotguns."

"Shells in both barrels. It's ready to go."

"You got an extra flashlight?" he asked.

I pulled my spare torch from beneath the kitchen sink, checked the batteries. I watched while he walked into the darkness. Bailey ran past me and both she and Mule walked beside him across the small field. Even if I hadn't been privy to the conversation at La Fonda that night, I'd know this character was innocent by the way Bailey and my neighbors accepted him. My ex-husband wasn't a bad person, but I recalled how they never visited Dana the few times he'd come around here. Dana pointed that out.

Chapter Twelve

Easter arrived, the snow had melted, and still no more surprises from the mystery man. Couldn't say I was glad because Dunlap was making plans to head back to Oklahoma, resume his life driving livestock haulers, leaving me here to solve the case alone. Of course the cops all said they'd work on the case, too, but I knew their budgets would not offer much help.

Dunlap had been interviewed by Shaw and a couple of Suits, polygraphed by the Suits, and cleared at the end of the day. I'd had to put up with a loud lecture from Detective Shaw who first suggested I'd done something illegal.

"What exactly was the illegal part?" I asked him.

"You gave sanctuary to Dunlap."

"I gave first aide to an injured victim."

"You didn't know that, at the time."

"Yeah, I did know that," I said.

"Intuition and hunches aren't worth much if they're wrong." Dunlap huffed.

"Not only was I correct about Dunlap," I reminded Shaw, "I was correct about the killer." DNA on both cigarettes matched, but they didn't have the perp's DNA on file. Still a mystery.

Shaw believed he'd persuaded me they kept an eye on similar cases across the nation. He said the feds were keeping lids on most of the information because that's what they did. A known pattern, over half a dozen dead women. Come to find out, two of the previous case evidence lists included same brand unlit cigarettes found at the abduction locations. Unfortunately, the only two with DNA were the two here in New Mexico.

Shaw said they kept these investigations quiet because it would upset too many people all across the nation if they knew how many of these psychopaths were still at large. Seemed to me the more people knew, the more they'd know what to be cautious about. Shaw said it didn't work that way. He said most of the people would be paranoid, and the rest would be vigilantes. He said vigilantes caused more harm than good.

A light knock on my door brought me out of my thoughts. "C'mon in, Dunlap."

"I'm packed up and ready to roll," he said, walking into the kitchen and taking a seat at the counter.

"Amtrak station in Albuquerque is a two hour drive. Your train doesn't leave for another five hours. You wanna go that early?"

"I'd like to buy you a nice dinner," Dunlap said.

"Thanks," I said. I thought of making a joke about the last woman he took to dinner not faring so well, but decided against it. "I'd enjoy a nice dinner."

"You have a preference?" he asked.

"Sure. There's an old hacienda restaurant in Old Town. Not far from the Amtrak station. Excellent New Mexican style food. Sound okay?"

"Works for me," he said.

"You hang here with Bailey while I find something else to wear."

I picked Dana's Christmas gift off my counter and walked slowly down the hall cradling the bowl. Dunlap was leaving to get on with his life. I'd grown accustomed to having him around. Because of Dunlap, Dana's lights were always on at night. I'd have to get used to the quiet darkness from her house all over again. Sam and Kopeki enjoyed hanging out with him at Dana's. I could be sure those two would soon be back at my place.

After a quick shower, I picked black wool slacks, a red turtleneck sweater, and a bright multicolored silk vest Dana gave me for my last birthday not long before she died. I'd not worn the birthday vest since I'd yet to have anywhere festive to wear it. Oddly after slipping it over my sweater I was reminded of the colorful velvet vests always sported by Dana's kindly hospice doctor. My face smiled and I realized I was beginning to replace the deep despairing grief with happy memories. My cousin would approve. "I'll always be with you," she'd promised. And she tapped the side of her head in the general area of her left temporal lobe, this being the place of stored memories.

"Let's get this show on the road," I spoke into the kitchen and den area. Dunlap sat on the raised hearth, Bailey at his feet. He'd stoked the fireplace with several logs and replaced the fire screen.

"Never saw you in anything but jeans and shirts," he said. "You clean up pretty good."

"Thanks," I said.

"You should get out more," he offered.

I shrugged. Left to my own devices I'd turn into a classic hermit. "Staying home keeps me out of the bars," I joked.

He carried his small duffel, one I'd given him, to my car. We crawled inside and followed the headlights to Old Town in Albuquerque.

"Your comment about staying out of the bars," Dunlap began. "You had a problem, a drinking problem?"

"Have," I corrected.

"You still drinking?"

"Not in recent years but I will always have a problem with alcohol."

"My father had more than a problem," he said.

"Yeah. I remember you mentioning that."

"Beat the hell out of me and my brothers. Have no idea what happened to them. He drank himself to death and they were older. They left, never came back. My mother died, like your cousin. Cancer. I was thirteen. Tried foster homes, but living on the streets was less dangerous."

"Hard way to live. I know. I've been there, too."

"I wondered," he said. "You sport a thick hide."

"You like Matchbox 20?" I asked, preferring a new topic.

"Can't beat Rob Thomas."

I slid one of their CD's into my player and we sang along. Neither of us could carry a tune. We arrived into a parking lot near the Old Town Plaza two CD's later.

"Going to miss you and your neighbors," Dunlap said as we strolled down sidewalks past numerous gift shops en route to the restaurant.

"We're gonna miss you, too. Hope you'll stop by when you're this way."

"I'll be back this way. My hauls take me through Albuquerque at least twice a month."

We arrived in the lobby and didn't have to wait. The evening patrons were few so our waitress seated us beside the tree.

"Looks like a tree growing right out of the roof," Dunlap remarked.

"It is."

"What happens if it rains or snows?"

"They sit us somewhere else," I laughed.

We ordered vegetarian combination plates. I'd learned a few things about Dunlap, one being when given a choice, he preferred not eating meat. Said he'd gotten to know too many hamburgers, as he called them, referring to the cattle he hauled. Said he just didn't feel right about killing animals anymore.

"You ever get to know cattle?" he asked me.

I thought back to the cattle around my ranch in central New Mexico. Specifically I remembered the mother cow who died after a difficult breach birth. Her calf survived and was adopted by another mother cow who already had a calf. I glanced over at Dunlap. "I have met a few," I said.

We enjoyed our cheese enchiladas, frijoles, Spanish rice, and sopapillas, and shared a chocolate raspberry cheesecake for dessert. Stuffed and cheered by good food and good company, we left Old Town, arriving at the Amtrak station approximately fifteen minutes before Dunlap's train left. He had just enough time to grab his ticket and board the Amtrak. I watched from the parking lot while the train pulled out from the station and moved down the track until it completely disappeared from view.

New Mexico Indians lined the station sidewalks peddling jewelry and crafts. I paused to inspect some of the jewelry while walking back to my car, and then I drove back to Old Town. The stores and shops would close within an hour, but I had time to visit a few. Dana and I had pottery in two gift shops here, and although I'd received generous checks from both for pieces they sold during December, I had not visited either since last autumn.

This evening I did not want to think of our pottery. I wanted to buy gifts for my neighbors. I purchased a few new heavy blankets. One for Bailey and one for Kopeki. Kopeki seated himself on normal furniture unless a blanket was handy, and then he would spread it across the floor and sit legs and arms akimbo. I found a Lobo football cap for Ben, who could truly care less about the actual team. Ben enjoyed the cartoonish wolf embroidered over the hat's brim. I found a wildly colorful Western shirt for Sam and a tortoise hair comb for Nakani. For some odd reason, Mule enjoyed wearing huge sombreros during hot summer days. Of course, Dana always cut holes out for his ears, which kept the sombrero in place on his big head. I thought he looked hilarious, but she'd scolded me more than once, told me I would hurt his feelings. Before continuing shopping for the sombrero, I deposited these items in my car.

The last shop I visited was one which also had two of our best bowls on display in their window. I avoided looking at the bowls because I knew I needed to attend to our pottery business, as I had completely ignored it since my cousin's death. Dana usually took care of the business side of our pottery sales. She discussed with store owners what sold best, which pieces we needed to replenish, and she helped in their display presentations.

This was my favorite shop because they always had the most interesting variety of typical New Mexican merchandise. They also had the perfect giant sombrero for Mule. Next to the sombreros a rack displayed delicate silk scarfs and vests. So here is where Dana found my birthday gift.

"These are one of a kind." Sally, the proprietor, walked up behind me. "A woman who lives in Estancia weaves the fabric by hand, and she uses her special fabrics to make these. She also makes jackets. We call it fabric art. Unique works of art. How are you, Myra?"

"I'm doing okay, Sally," I replied. "As you can see, I already have the vest."

She showed me several of the other vests and scarfs. They were quite pricey, but exquisitely beautiful. I selected a scarf which coordinated with my vest.

"You want me to package it, or would you like to wear it?" she asked.

"I'll wear it," I said, wrapping the soft brightly colored fabric art once around my neck, allowing the long ends to drape over my shoulder.

"How is Dana?" Sally asked while I paid for the scarf and sombrero.

"I've been meaning to phone her. We sold out everything but the two most expensive bowls during Christmas. We could use more of the usual assortment."

I forgot that I had not contacted this store, nor the other one here in Old Town, to let them know my cousin was gone. "Dana passed away in November," I said. "She had cancer."

"Oh my goodness! I really had no idea! I wondered why she hadn't stopped in. I hadn't seen or heard from her in five months. I have missed seeing her! I am so sorry!"

"I am the one who is sorry. I do apologize, and I know this is awkward for you. I have not been away from home much since she died. I do have quite a nice new assortment of pottery, and I will bring it down within a few days."

"Oh my," Sally said again. "I just had no idea. I did notice she'd been losing a lot of weight, which showed because she was already so thin. But, well, you know, we just don't put these things together, and she never said a word."

"Dana wasn't big on words," I said.

"My deepest condolences. I am so very sorry. I'm sorry for myself, too. I will miss her visits and her pieces. Of course, we hope to continue selling your pieces."

"I'll call you in a few," I said. "And thank you for caring about her."

Sally turned her *Open* sign around to read *Closed* after I left the store. She had tears in her eyes. I felt bad that I had not shared the sad news with all who knew her. Etiquette is a class I would have certainly failed.

The next morning seemed like Christmas. Ben showed up and I gave him his University of New Mexico Lobo cap. He looked over the other gifts, left, and returned with everyone.

To my surprise, Nakani showed the most excitement. She fixed the new comb into her hair and could not stop removing and admiring it, and returning it to her hair. She hugged me several times before she disappeared. Sam, Kopeki, Ben, and Mule all thanked me and left together. I watched while they walked off toward the ruins. I'd cut two holes in Mule's hat and he wore it like a crown of jewels. Several times I noticed Sam and Kopeki making remarks to Mule. I knew they were telling him how grand he looked.

He held his head ever so proudly. Where in the world did he get the idea he should wear a sombrero? I shook my head and chuckled, then headed for the ceramic studio where I finished painting several pieces which had already been fired in the kiln.

CHAPTER THIRTEEN

Rick Bell, my old boss, published a midsize newspaper in Central New Mexico. He assigned me to interview Beau Haggis after Haggis chopped his young son to pieces with an ax some years earlier. I'd written for his newspaper until I sold my place and moved up here. Several times each year I still wrote articles, usually feature fluff for holidays, as Rick called them. I put Dunlap on the Amtrak in April. The following week I restocked both gift shops in Old Town with an assortment of pottery similar to what Dana would have provided. In early May I drove around to half a dozen smaller New Mexico communities, jotted down their planned parades and special events, then sent a nice fluffy Memorial Day story to Rick.

Keeping my days busy put me on the ascent out of grief. I'd almost forgotten about the Memorial Day article when my phone rang.

"Myra. Good piece. Loved it." Rick's voice echoed ulterior motive.

"It's filler fluff and you don't even read that stuff. What's up? You haven't called in years."

Rick quit waltzing and moved right to motive. "Remember the girl who burned to death up in your neck of the woods late last year?"

"The one killed on my property?"

"You're kidding! The first one was on your property?" Rick did seem surprised.

"That part was never mentioned in the news," I said.

"No," he chimed in. "No, they sure left that part out."

"What about it?"

"Wow. So that happened right there? Wow. Reason I'm calling is because it happened again. Woman found in the trunk of her burned out car this morning. Salt Lake City."

"Salt Lake City?" My mind ran around in circles trying to see how SLC fit in with the other crime cities. It didn't, according to my first impressions that locale had something to do with international hubs. SLC was not a hub city for anything I could think of.

"You didn't hear?" Rick asked.

"I've been busy in the ceramic studio. I haven't seen the news. What's your game, Rick?"

"You're the gal, Myra. I told myself this morning, Myra can work that story like no one else. Remember Haggis? We got syndication on your stories for that."

"Haggis is why I left crime coverage, Rick. I do have some interest in this serial case because I don't believe they'll ever find the guy . . . unless he falls down in front of the cops with a handful of accelerants and maps to all the crime scenes." I did not add that I was the one who made the serial connection. If I hadn't sent the anonymous note to Shaw, and cigarettes at both abduction sites hadn't got match hits on DNA, I wasn't convinced it would have ever been seen as a serial crime. I did not also add I'd had a few long talks with myself after Dunlap was cleared, and after I believed the mystery man was not returning to the crime scene on my property. I talked myself into leaving this one alone. I was not interested in another Haggis.

"You'd get a budget." Rick used his most persuasive tone. "You travel to several of the last out-of-state crime scenes, work interviews, you know. Do what you're good at, following your instincts."

"What kind of a budget?" I heard myself ask. I could not believe Rick was pulling me back in again.

"Plane fare, meals, bus fare."

"Whoa! Bus fare?"

"For getting around when you get there."

"Forget that," I said.

"Okay. Taxi fare."

"Not good enough."

"You know we can't afford rental cars, too."

"You want me to do this story?"

"Myra, you're trying to rob us here."

"Bus routes run just that, routes. Taxis leave you at a destination spot. You want another ride, you call another taxi. I'm not spending half my time changing buses or calling taxis."

"Okay. Let me go over our expense budget. I'll call you back in a few."

"A few what, Rick. Days? Hours?"

"Hours."

I hung up my phone.

Rick called back within the hour.

"How about this," he began, "use your car for Denver. That's what, a five or six hour drive? And Salt Lake City isn't that much farther. We'll pay gas, hotel, food. You pick the other two crime scenes, we'll pick up plane fare and rental car. But no more than three days on the rental. You pay hotel and food in those two places."

"I'll get back to you," I said. Rick and I never communicated until we hung up on each other at least twice for each assignment. I made a cup of tea and watched out the window while Ben chased the Haggis rabbit with a stick. Bailey soaked up rays from sunlight which poured through French doors in my den. I considered waking her when the phone rang again.

"Okay, okay," Rick said. "Plane fare to two crime scene cities, meals and a rental to Denver and Salt Lake City."

"I'm supposed to pick up my own hotel bill?"

"Myra, you know what our budget looks like. We can't swing the whole enchilada."

"Let me sleep on it," I said.

"Don't hang up."

"I didn't. I said let me sleep on it."

"I'll be up later today," he said. "We'll sort out the particulars."

"Thanks for the flowers," I said.

"Sorry?"

"The flowers for Dana," I said. "Never wrote you a thank you. They were beautiful. She loved them."

"I liked your cousin," he said. "I'm truly sorry she left us." With that, he closed the line.

Rick had sent a huge basket with a mixture of every flower color imaginable. It arrived the second day of Dana's hospice stay. I was surprised by his kindness to a person he'd only met a handful of times and glad he hadn't waited to send it on the third day. She was sitting up talking with me that second morning when the flowers were carried into her room. Sandy sent her an equally lovely arrangement which arrived the same day of Dana's admit into hospice. These were the only adieus she received, and she appreciated them more than anything I could have imagined. She would die there, that she knew, and these tokens of compassion touched her deeply. When she could no longer notice the flowers, I was comforted by and grateful for them. There is no place more lonely than a hospice room, except perhaps the hospice room which echoes from emptiness when one has been forgotten by all.

I stuck my head out my kitchen door and called Ben. He threw his stick down and ran over to see me.

"My old boss will be here today. I wonder if you could make sure the Haggis rabbit doesn't come anywhere near the houses?"

"Okay," he said cheerfully while turning his University of New Mexico Lobo's cap around backward. He grabbed his stick and sent the Haggis rabbit over the distant hill.

"Good. One less thing I don't have to explain."

I ran the vacuum throughout my house, emptied my dishwasher, and started a nice pot of green chili while I pressure cooked pinto beans. While everything simmered I mixed up my favorite yellow cornbread. Rick would enjoy the meal and I would relish the company.

Except for Bailey, infrequent surprise visits from Rudy, and occasional visits from my neighbors, my world was silent unless I chose to talk to myself. Not that I didn't do that more than could be considered healthy these days, but I preferred a nice visit with someone who could relate to my life in this world, and who could occupy space without disappearing.

Dunlap promised he'd return. Nearly two months went by and I did not hear from him. I wondered if he'd lost his job hauling livestock.

While removing cornbread from the oven, I heard what sounded like a train coming at my house. Tossing the pan on the counter I hurried outside.

Dunlap had pulled his empty livestock hauler up alongside my carport, making my Toyota and Dana's old GMC pickup seem like tinker toys beside a Tonka Truck.

"You son-of-a-bitch!" I said, hugging my friend. "Where the hell have you been? I thought you'd lost your job!"

"I did," he grinned. "But I hired on with a big ranch up in Wichita. Now I don't haul hamburgers. I transfer herds through Texas and Kansas."

"What does that mean, transfer herds?"

"Rancher moves 'em where he gets grazing permits. Most of the cattle I haul are mother cows. They don't kill 'em. Pretty cool, huh?" Dunlap grinned like a kid describing his new job in a bubble gum store. "They sold a load of young mother cows to a ranch near Grants. I delivered 'em this morning."

"Uh oh," I remembered Rick would show up any moment.

"I don't like uh oh's," Dunlap lost his smile.

The feds knew Dunlap would be targeted by the serial killer. Dunlap's resurrection had been kept secret by the cops and the feds. I couldn't reveal any of this to a newspaper man, my old boss, Rick. They hadn't concealed his identity, but since Dunlap had no family looking for him, the cops left it alone. "You're gonna have to role play," I said. "The publisher and editor of a newspaper I used to write for is showing up. You're gonna have to be a boyfriend. He knows my only family is a niece."

"Okay." Dunlap's grin returned. "I can do boyfriend."

"Remember, less is more. Follow anything I say. Don't add. Just follow."

As we turned toward the house, Rick Bell pulled up and parked beside the livestock hauler. He jumped out of his green Chevy Tahoe and walked around the big truck. We waited for him to complete his inspection, then I introduced him.

"Rick, this is my good friend, Jim." I said the first name that came to mind.

"Nice to meet you." Dunlap shook Rick's hand.

"You're a truck driver." Rick stated the obvious.

"Yes, Sir."

"Well, we need truck drivers." Rick smiled.

Bailey rushed passed us when we entered the kitchen. She disappeared in the direction of the old ruins, probably in search of Ben since I could see

Mule over near Dana's adobe. I was immediately glad I'd asked Ben to keep the Haggis rabbit away from both houses.

"Cornbread's warm and chili's ready," I offered. "Pick a place at the table and let me serve us up something good to eat."

"You didn't have to fix dinner," Rick protested mildly.

"You drove all the way up here at dinner time," I winked. "Besides, it's nice to have company at the table."

"Smells great," Dunlap added.

I sent both men off to different bathrooms to wash up. They returned walking down the hallway together looking like a couple of old buddies. I picked up bits of their conversation. Dunlap described the work of handling large animals, making sure they were always treated with care, making sure sick animals didn't end up trampled in the livestock hauler by healthier animals. Rick seemed interested. They took seats at the dinning room table, where I'd already set linen place mats and napkins, and placed a platter of cornbread. I carried the steamy bowls of chili to each guest, offered ice tea and lemonade, then sat with them. We dropped conversation for a few minutes and simply enjoyed the good food.

"So, Corey Dunlap," Rick said with a grin while I made coffee. "How'd you get messed up with all this?"

I stared over the counter at both men. Dunlap sat with a blank expression.

"You knew all along," I snapped.

Rick nodded. "You forgot his photo was on the television once or twice."

"Yeah, like what, six months ago? You remembered?"

"Old newspaper man like me, we never forget a mug shot."

"Don't think I ever had a mug shot," Dunlap protested.

"He's never had a mug shot," I added.

"I don't mean it like that." Rick sounded apologetic. "I just meant his mug was on television. It was a head shot ... on television."

"I get it," I said sarcastically. "Cops aren't saying anything one way or the other about Dunlap," I said, "for obvious reasons."

"Besides security camera tapes, you're the only witness." Rick looked at Dunlap.

"Guess I am the only real live witness."

I stared at Dunlap and wondered what he meant by *real live witness*. Nah. He couldn't possibly have figured out Ben wasn't a live person. I studied his face for a few moments.

"Don't sweat this," Rick said. "I'm not breathing a word."

"Thanks," I said.

Mule usually vanished after the sun went down, but I could see his big nose pressed up against the window behind Rick. Dunlap saw him, too.

"Mule's spying on us." Dunlap mentioned the obvious.

Rick swung around to meet Mule's big brown eyes. "What's on his head?"

"His hat," I said. I had no idea why Mule enjoyed eavesdropping. Dana said he'd always been that way. I wondered if he understood what people said.

"You ever going to give me the whole story?" Rick asked.

I was having another thought. "Rick, I'm back with the paper, right?"

"Right."

"I want autopsy reports for all the vics we know about." Medical investigators would provide autopsy reports to newspaper reporters. Not to individuals unless they were family members. "Can you call for those first thing tomorrow morning?"

"Sure," Rick said. "Medical investigators will charge us about twenty dollars per report. It'll come out of your working budget. You got my interest. What's up?"

"Can you ask them to fax the reports right away?"

"I can do that."

"And you'll fax those to me soon as you get them?"

"Of course. Myra. What's going through your head?"

"Yeah," Dunlap agreed. "What're you talking about?"

"Autopsy reports show what happened to the victim," I said. "How they died."

"They were all burned to death." Dunlap sounded confused.

"Maybe not," I said.

"Okay," Rick said. "You're the biologist. What're you thinking?"

"Veronica North was alive when he set the car on fire," I said. "His whole routine was altered by you." I glanced at Dunlap.

"Whattaya mean?" Dunlap asked, then turned to me.

"Mystery man didn't know she wasn't alone," I said. "She fit his plan, then you showed up. Ruined the plan."

"I'm not following." Dunlap said.

"She's got a degree in biology," Rick said. "She understands a lot of the stuff they look at in forensics. You're wondering how many of the vics were alive and how many were already dead, aren't you? Autopsy records will tell you. So far, every old news article I've seen says the vics were burned in their own car trunks. Not much more information. Alive at time of death, or dead. You want to know the details. Are we sure North was alive when the car burned?"

"I know she was," Dunlap interrupted.

I already knew she was alive, too. Ben said she screamed while he tried to open the trunk.

"What next, Myra?" Rick asked.

"Get the autopsy reports ASAP. I want those before I do anything."

"I don't understand much of this conversation," Dunlap said. "What should I do?"

Rick and I both turned to stare at Dunlap. "You better hope that creep has no idea where you are," Rick said. "You're a pretty consistently moving target. That's probably good."

"I got me a rifle," Dunlap said. "I carry that in the truck when I'm on the road."

"Looks like my work is over and I can go home." Rick dismissed us with a grin.

I shrugged. By initiating the autopsy reports through the newspaper, I was on the assignment. It wasn't quite done for me. "We haven't completely agreed upon my expenses."

"You get rental cars anywhere for up to three days. After three days, you're on your own with rental fees. You get hotel for up to three days. After three days, you're on your own with hotel expenses. You get to pay for your own meals. Hey, you don't eat much, Myra. You can swing the food. Besides, you eat anyway whether you're working or home."

"What about plane fare?" I asked.

"Plane fare to two cities. Rental cars to two cities."

I stood up, Rick stood up, and we shook hands. One thing I'd learned about Rick many years ago, a handshake was his bond. He didn't always stick to written agreements, but he did stay true to those sealed with a handshake.

"Enjoyed meeting you, Corey," Rick said. "I-40 runs through Moriarty, you know. Next time you get to New Mexico, I'll buy you dinner. Deal?"

"Deal," Dunlap said.

"I like this guy," Rick said. "He's easy to get along with."

While Rick drove home to Moriarty, Dunlap helped me load dishes into the dishwasher. "You want to stay in Dana's house this evening?" I asked.

"I'm way off route up here," he said. "I delivered my haul this morning and was supposed to make it back to Wichita tonight. If I get back on the road I can make it home before morning."

"You think you'll be this way again any time soon?"

"I just drive the trucks," Dunlap said. "I don't make the routes."

"Keep in touch. And keep that rifle close. We don't know who this guy is, where he lives, or where he'll show up next."

"What's your plan?"

"Not sure. I think after I read the autopsy reports I'll have a clue. Don't know, really. Just know there's something in those reports that will open this up more."

"Oh, hey. Almost forgot to tell you." Dunlap grinned and let me wonder.

"Out of guesses. What?"

"I bought me a twenty-six foot trailer. Now I just gotta buy a truck to pull it."

"What kind of trailer?"

"The box that carries cargo. You know, the big box with wheels you see behind eighteen wheelers."

"You gonna branch out and be your own trucker?" I asked.

"Hope so. In fact, I was gonna ask if I could drop the trailer here until I get my truck. Rancher in Wichita charges me storage to park it at his place."

"Sure. Park it over the other side of Dana's place. It'll be out of the way there."

Bailey and Ben returned. Mule had never left.

"I kept the Haggis rabbit busy," Ben said, proud of himself.

"You did a good job." I smiled and winked at Ben.

"What's the Haggis rabbit?" Dunlap asked.

"He's bad," Ben said. "Rudy turned him into … "

"Rudy messed him up a bit," I interrupted.

"Rudy's one big wolf. Surprised he didn't just eat the rabbit."

Dunlap visited with Ben for a short while, admired Mule's sombrero, scratched Bailey's head, then aimed his livestock hauler toward Santa Fe en route home to Wichita.

Chapter Fourteen

"Is your fax on?" Rick asked soon as I picked the phone up two days later.

"It will be. You got the autopsy reports?"

"Got four of them."

"You read them?"

"Briefly," he said. "You were right. Some real interesting information. Okay. I'm sending these over in about ten minutes. By the way, got a couple of pre morbid photos of the vics in Denver and Los Angeles. You're going to be interested. Compare them to the vics here in New Mexico. Wide range in ages, but there's a resemblance."

I hung up and switched on my color fax, selected its highest resolution quality, then waited. Soon as the light blinked and the whirring began, the reports and photos printed out.

Denver, Los Angeles, Seattle, and Minneapolis. Excellent. These varied in years since incidents and carried back a decade. There were two photographs. Rick was correct. Veronica North, the victim in Los Lunas, Denver and Los Angeles all had physical characteristics in common: Petite, similar in weight, facial features, hair style, and hair color. They also had what I would call athletic builds. These women either frequented gyms, or they exercised on home equipment. Made me think of something Ben said about the killer. He could run fast. Really fast. He had to be an athlete, and this was making sense. I didn't know how, yet, but it made sense.

I set the photographs aside and read the reports. Denver and LA didn't have smoke or chemicals caused by the fire in their lungs. That meant they were dead before they were burned. I didn't have good information about Los Lunas. News reports indicated she was burned beyond recognition. One story indicated cause of death was not known. Until I read the autopsy I would assume she was dead before the car burned. All four women did not wear wedding rings. Interesting. I thought back to the store clerk in Los Lunas. The mystery man had targeted her, and I didn't recall much about her except she was waiting for her husband, which is what saved her from being a victim. Did she wear a wedding ring? I'd never worn my ring when I was married. It was possible this data was important and not simply co-incidence.

I was tall and thin and my hair was mixed with about twenty percent gray these days. I did not resemble these women in any way. Still, I rummaged through an old box, found my wedding ring and slipped it on. I was going in search of this serial killer. He obviously had a type he targeted. I would be the opposite.

Logging into my online bank account, I noted Rick had already sent a direct deposit to my account. My expenses above this amount would be reimbursed for the most part. Next I called a car rental agency that delivered their cars. While I waited I packed a suitcase and checked my laptop. I also set aside Bailey's favorite blanket, dog food, feeding dishes, and several gallons of bottled water. I called the American Automobile Association and got a list of hotels in and around Denver that allowed pets.

Within a couple of hours Bailey and I were on the road.

After two days interviewing people the Denver vic knew I believed I'd discovered a new similarity with the New Mexico vics. They were considered average by their peers and they lacked education beyond high school, which would've probably showed up in their vocabularies. All three worked full time in jobs with no future. They all drove low end cars and lived in modest apartments. In addition to all their other matching traits, these women spent the bulk of their income on appearance. Flashy department store clothes, heavy on the makeup and good haircuts. They also maintained memberships in health clubs.

Middling and unsophisticated, but lots of attention to the package.

I paid such little attention to the cashier in Los Lunas who could have been the target that night. However, I was sure she'd had blonde hair, and she was neither athletic nor flashy. So that put a new spin on the mystery man's targets. He did pick them, they weren't random. That night the cashier waited for her husband while the mystery man waited for his next victim, and it wasn't her.

This serial killer had a specific woman in mind. Petite but athletic, short stylish brunette hair, lots of makeup, unmarried, poorly employed, and poorly educated. Might be a reason he preferred this profile, and there might not. Psychopaths were an anomalous group. As often as they'd been categorized and studied I did not believe anyone understood what made them tick. Haggis was my example. He lived an apparent ordinary existence until he killed his family. However, I did not believe he'd ever been ordinary. I believe he was a monster all his life. No one made him that way. Monsters are born. My opinion.

This particular monster would be no different. According to Dunlap and Ben he fit the Haggis age range. Of course, he didn't suddenly emerge on the homicide scene. This guy had been carefully selecting his victims for more than a decade. My guess is he'd been doing this a lot longer than ten years. Probably most of his life.

"You hungry?" I asked Bailey who sat shotgun.

"Hhwmm," Bailey said.

I pulled into a fast food drive-through and bought myself a big chef salad, and three hamburger patties for Bailey. She ate her hamburgers while I picked through the salad.

"We'll be home for dinner," I told her. She settled down in the passenger seat with her head on her front paws.

Slipping an audio book into the CD player, I decided not to obsess anymore this day. I'd learned distraction from Dana. Distraction was a form of quiet time and turned out to be a tool I relied upon. Distraction helped me stay sober, helped me feel okay about myself.

"Maybe your mind can't be quiet," Dana noted soon after I sold my ranch and moved in with her while my new home was under construction. "You need quiet time."

"What's quiet time?" I'd asked.

"Quiet time is like distracting yourself."

"Distracting myself from what?" I asked.

"You can't stand empty space. Everything has to be filled up."

"You're probably right."

"What do you think about when you aren't actually doing something?" Dana asked.

"Not sure."

"Buy a spiral notebook," she said.

"Okay. Then what?"

"I will show you what you spend your time thinking."

"What'll that accomplish?" I asked.

"You'll see."

I remember being so curious I drove to Santa Fe and purchased several spiral notebooks, drove back to Dana's, interrupted her afternoon in the ceramic studio, and talked her into demonstrating how a simple notebook could help. Kopeki and Sam had been drinking coffee while watching a fifty year old rerun of Bonanza. Dana turned the television off and we all sat in a circle on her living room floor. Kopeki could neither read nor write, and he was entirely confused by the exercise. Sam sat there perfectly quiet and smiled the whole while.

"Write down what you just thought," Dana said.

I opened the notebook and stared at the blank page.

"What did you think?" she demanded. "Just now. Right there. That thought. I see you have a thought. What is it? Write it down."

I put my pen to paper and found myself writing critical things about myself. I filled up one page, and then the second page, and the third page. Dana took my spiral and read.

"Your thoughts are insulting to yourself. You tell yourself insults about yourself."

"Maybe I'm just bored," I said.

"Do you have thoughts like this all the time?" Dana asked.

I considered the question. "Probably."

"How many thoughts do you think you have in one day?"

I shrugged.

"Hundreds," Dana said. "And if most of your thoughts are like these, no wonder you drink. You insult yourself. Your insults make you feel bad. Right?"

"Well," I said. "Yeah. I guess. So you say I'm talking myself into misery?"

"Whatever you say in your mind. Your thoughts. Those things you think. If you fill up your empty time insulting yourself, how can you not be miserable?"

"It's how my mind works."

"No," she said. "You control your own thoughts. Take these spirals with you. When you catch yourself feeling unhappy, or mad, or upset, you know, bad feelings, write down what you are talking yourself into. Write down your thoughts. Then practice not insulting yourself. Practice saying respectful things to yourself. Turn your thoughts into respectful thinking. Not insults. Okay?"

"How does that teach me quiet meditation time?"

"When you aren't busy, you are keeping your mind busy with thoughts that make you uncomfortable. Where is the quiet time? If you turn your uncomfortable thoughts into comfortable thoughts, you will start enjoying the times when you aren't busy because you won't feel uncomfortable with all that open space in your day. Your quiet time will feel more comfortable, and you will learn to enjoy it."

Now, while I drove the rental car across the Colorado State Line into New Mexico, I smiled. I'd quickly gone through a dozen spiral notebooks writing down the things that went through my mind. I learned that I was an expert at talking myself into feeling mad, bad, sad, lonely, stupid, worthless, and about a hundred other insults. By writing these things down I became aware of my thoughts. Through awareness, I learned to change my own thinking. When the thinking changed, I did begin to enjoy quiet time because I did not use it to harm myself with my own thoughts.

Dana was correct. I gradually learned to like my own company. I discovered I did not feel the urge to drink. Drinking had always helped me avoid myself, had always filled up quiet time. Such a wise person, my cousin.

My choice of this particular book turned out perfect. The story ended a few minutes before I turned off the highway and drove down the long dirt road to my carport.

"Dunlap dropped off his trailer," I noted.

Bailey jumped up and barked at the large box. I parked in my carport, glanced across the field at the top of the box, which did show a few inches above Dana's adobe. Bailey sprang from the car and ran off to inspect this new giant yard ornament while I unloaded our travel paraphernalia and carried it into my house.

Spring evenings bargained with the sun, kept it afloat in the sky hours beyond early winter nightfall. I had plenty of time to unpack and take a long hot bath, which I did right away. Later I washed and dried Bailey's food and water bowls, filled them, set them in their usual place beside the pantry, slipped on shoes and a light jacket, and set out to inspect Dunlap's tractor trailer box.

The back doors were open and I was not surprised to discover Mule, Ben and Bailey in the trailer. A refrigerator unit attached in the front, and I was impressed at how thick the walls were, how shiny and clean everything appeared.

"What're you doing in there?" I had to ask.

"My good friend Corey told me to take care of his box," Ben announced. Ben had placed blankets on the floor surface and logs for sitting, creating the atmosphere of a child's clubhouse.

Bailey collapsed in a happy heap on the blankets, Ben was seated on one of the logs, and Mule, wearing his sombrero, stood lookout beside the open doors. I crawled up inside and sat upon the other log. "Comfy cozy," I remarked.

"The box can turn into winter," Ben stated proudly.

I nodded. "Yes. This is a refrigerated trailer. Our friend Dunlap can haul frozen foods with this, as soon as he has a truck to pull it."

Mule turned around and now stood with his big head right next to my face. For the first time ever, I realized Mule did not have any odor. Mules and horses always smelled like a mixture of sweet sweat and dirt. Mule didn't smell like anything. And, he didn't attract flies, either. I wondered why I'd never thought this before. It made me wonder if Dunlap had ever noticed this.

Bailey barked and the sound bounced off the inside metal walls. When the echoes ceased I heard a tickity-tickity-tickity racket which seemed to come from the outside top of the trailer. I jumped down and ran around to the front of the box where I'd seen a ladder fixed against the side leading up to the refrigerator unit. I climbed up and discovered Rooster and the Happy Hens. They were pecking and scratching away. I guessed they wanted corn, so I fetched several cans full of the treat from the bins in my storage shed.

"This is the best room I ever had," Ben said when I eventually returned to his clubhouse. Bailey was sound asleep and Mule pretended to be asleep.

"Don't get too attached," I cautioned. "Dunlap is going to haul this thing around the country earning his living."

Ben seemed unaffected by my words of caution and I left him and Bailey and Mule to enjoy their new metal clubhouse.

I prepared a bowl of clam chowder and a cup of hot tea, then began sorting and categorizing my notes from Denver.

CHAPTER FIFTEEN

I waited a week before calling the rental agency, then asked them to deliver another car to my door. Repeating my routine to get ready, I loaded the rental and headed for Salt Lake City with Bailey sitting shotgun once again.

There was definitely a pattern to his selections.

With one new twist.

The victim worked as a records clerk in a school administration office. Basically, she entered information into computer files. I interviewed the vic's coworkers and couldn't help but notice one of the women could have been a selection.

"Were you good friends with the victim?" I asked her.

"I've only worked here three months," she said. "I didn't know her that well."

"You are aware you looked alike?"

The woman shrugged. "We used the same hair stylist."

"You go to the same health club?"

"Health club? No. I've never been to a health club. Several of us who work here use the school's gym. It's one of the perks for working here. End of the day we can work out in the gym until the janitors lock up. We're all trying to lose a few pounds, you know. Exercise helps."

"A couple of your coworkers said some of you went for dinner the night the victim was killed." Unless the mystery man pre targeted his latest victim, he could have easily picked this other woman from that group. The victim was in her early thirties. This woman was probably late thirties.

Neither were married, neither had children. I asked her if she saw a man that night in the restaurant who fit Ben and Dunlap's description of the mystery man.

"No," she said. "I don't remember anyone like that at the restaurant. But I've seen the person you're talking about. I'm not sure where."

"You've seen him? How often?"

"I don't know," she said. "Like I said, I'm not even sure where I've seen him. But the person you described seems familiar."

I studied her face. Each time I asked her to recall something, her eyes glanced to the left. Not exactly a science, but when people are telling a story, trying to find pieces to fill in what they don't remember, their eyes look to the right. If it's all fabrication, they glance to the left.

"If you see him again," I said, "or if you remember where you've seen this man, this is my card. Call me collect." I took out a pen and jotted down Rick's number, as well. "I've included a second phone number," I said. "It's the newspaper I write for. If you can't reach me, there's always someone answering their phones."

With this new tangle, I knew I should do something, but what?

After our interview, I stopped by a public park and let Bailey run off some energy. When we returned to the hotel I dialed the number on Shaw's card.

"Shaw speaking."

"Myra Whitehawk here," I said. "Do you remember me?"

"Of course, Myra. How can I help you?"

"I'm working on research," I began, "for a story on that serial killer."

"Where is this research taking you?" he asked.

I knew what he meant, but I answered the question my way. "Right now it's got me in Salt Lake City. Just talked to the people who worked with the most recent victim. One of those women resembles all the women who've been killed."

"And your meaning is what?"

"What if he comes back here? What if he targets this other person?"

"You realize those odds are slim."

"No," I said. "I don't realize that. I'm suggesting this is new. And she recalls seeing him."

"How does she know that?"

"I have Dunlap's description, a store clerk's description, and what we all saw on the security tapes. She said she's seen him. She doesn't know where." I didn't include that she was probably holding back, or outright fabricating, part of her recollection. I sensed, however, this mystery man was a threat. How? No clue.

"I'll call the detective in charge up there, give him this information," Shaw said.

"Thanks."

"Myra," Shaw said.

"Yes?"

"I am familiar with how close you came to getting killed doing this once before. You got smarter since then, right?"

"I got sober," I said.

"Sober's a good thing."

After hanging up I wondered if my concerns were paranoid. Paranoia couldn't hurt. I gathered up my stuff and checked out. Really wasn't any reason to stay another night.

"We're gonna get home after midnight," I told Bailey.

Bailey didn't care. Her doggy expression said, "Let's go home, now."

Early summer is beautiful, especially driving the Four Corners. That's where Utah, Arizona, Colorado, and New Mexico have common borders. Technically you could put each hand and each foot in a state and be in four states at once. Unfortunately by the time we crossed the four corner region it was too dark to even see what existed outside the car windows. Bailey snored and I slipped an audio book into the CD player.

* * *

The driveway passed by Dana's adobe before ending at my carport. Although the hour was very late Mule stood beside Dunlap's box trailer, which struck me as unusual. After parking the rental beside my carport, Bailey and I walked across the field, around the adobe, and discovered Mule wasn't alone. Rooster and the Happy Hens perched along the edges of the top to the trailer.

"Why are you guys out here so late?" I asked Mule. Mule shook his head, which caused his sombrero to fall off. I picked up the big hat, slipped his ears through the holes, and arranged it back in place. Suddenly Bailey growled, then launched into her crazy dog routine, barking, growling, having a fit. Loud noises came from inside the box. Luckily the moon was bright and I could see the latches. Unfastening them, I opened the trailer.

"What in the world?" I heard myself say. The Haggis rabbit, bloody from banging itself around inside the trailer, jumped out and raced off into the night's darkness.

Rooster and the Happy Hens flew down from their place of perch. Together with Mule they all left in the direction of the ancient ruins.

I shrugged and hurried home, too tired to even be curious.

The next morning I would have slept until noon if the phone hadn't interrupted me.

"Hello?"

"Is this Myra Whitehawk?" a woman asked.

"Yes." My caller ID showed the number was blocked.

"I talked with you yesterday. You asked me to let you know if I remembered where I'd seen that man."

"And?"

"I know this sounds bizarre, but I think it was the 2002 Winter Olympics. They were here in Salt Lake City."

"Ten years ago," I said. "Does sound a little bizarre. How can you be sure?"

"I'm not sure, but I kept picking up this memory after I talked with you. There was this guy at the Olympics who kept following me around."

"Did you talk with him?"

"No. I was married in those days, and I was waiting for my husband. When my husband finally showed up, that guy disappeared."

"You are absolutely sure of this?"

"I am. I mean, I'm not sure it was the same guy. But he was kind of a show off. He was muscular."

"Athletic. Could he have been a participant in the Olympics?" I asked.

"He pretended to be, you know. Dressed like he was part of one of the teams. I'm not sure it was the same guy. But that memory just won't leave me alone."

"Did you look the same?" I asked.

"No. I was much younger."

"Did you wear the same hair style? Same hair color? Stuff like that. And your wedding ring, did you wear one?"

"I don't remember how I wore my hair, but the color is still the same. And no, I never had a wedding ring. I've told you all I recall," she said.

"I appreciate your letting me know this," I said. "And you know my phone number. If you think of anything … "

"I'll call you again," she interrupted. And then she hung up.

The 2002 Winter Olympics, Salt Lake City, the mystery man was there. Because he lives there? He attends Winter Olympic events?

I researched the Winter Olympic sites for the past thirty years: Lake Placid, New York; Sarajevo, Yugoslavia; Calgary, Canada; Albertville, France; Lillehammer, Norway; Nagano, Japan; Salt Lake City, Utah; Turin, Italy. No similar murders during any of those times. Although I didn't really expect the Olympics to be part of any pattern, I was glad to eliminate them as a possible connection. Travel to any of those places would be out of my pocket expenses. Rick would never go for it.

This entire angle was probably a red herring. There's no way in the world I'd remember that I saw someone at an event, even if the person was known to me, ten years ago.

CHAPTER SIXTEEN

"When are you planning your flights?" Rick asked.

"I'm not sure what to do with Bailey," I said.

"Bring her to Moriarty. She can hang out with my dogs."

"If I can't come up with something, I'll take you up on that," I said.

We discussed all my findings and Rick wanted me to write a headline piece with just enough new information about the mystery man who'd recently struck in New Mexico that readers would buy up all his newspapers.

"I'll send an article over in the morning," I promised.

"Good work, Myra."

My travels in search of new information were costing Rick's paper a chunk of change and I wasn't sure what I'd write, but I did owe him a story.

That evening while I sorted out all my notes, records and photographs, it occurred to me I could use photographs of the four women showing their similarities. I wrote a short piece, mostly referencing that this killer seemed to prefer a specific type. I made notations where Rick could insert the photos, and then I hit the send button and let it fly off to Rick's computer. Within an hour he phoned. He loved it.

The next morning I took Bailey to Rick's house and he drove me to the airport. I caught a flight to Los Angeles. My interviews and record searches yielded all the same information. I caught a flight from LA to Seattle, and was not surprised to find almost the same material.

The mystery man had a type. Every one of his victims had similar life styles, similar employment, and very similar appearances. I did not doubt for one second that he didn't target the vics. There was no way he could arrive into a city and find a woman who met all his criteria during a day or two.

When I hunted down Haggis, I wanted to know why he killed his family. That was then. All these years later I didn't care why the mystery man killed, because caring what made him a serial killer didn't help future victims. My focus was the women he was selecting.

Rick picked me up at the Albuquerque airport upon my return. We drove to his home in Moriarty, I retrieved Bailey, had a cup of coffee while I gave him a condensed summation of my findings, and then I drove two and a half hours home.

Dunlap's livestock hauler sat empty beside the much shorter refrigerated box trailer. Bailey flew from the car and ran toward Dana's adobe. Although exhausted and feeling like visiting was the last thing on my mind, I headed that way, too.

"You're wearing glasses!" This being my first impression.

"I've had to wear distance glasses to drive for years," Dunlap grinned. "Finally was able to afford these. Now I can see close up and far away, all with the same lenses."

"When'd you get in?" I asked.

"Last night. I had a load of young cows. Delivered 'em to a ranch near Ramah."

"Glad you stopped by." I pointed at Rooster and the Happy Hens, who sat perched along the top of his box trailer. "You see your addition has gotten to be quite popular. By the way, where's Mule?"

"He took off over the hill with Bailey. Guess they're looking for Ben."

"They've all been up in your trailer," I confessed.

"That's okay," Dunlap grinned. He always had such a congenial attitude.

"I'm just back from Los Angeles and Seattle," I said. "Give me an hour to unpack and freshen up, then come on over for dinner."

"I've got salmon steaks," he offered.

"Salmon steaks? Wow. Those'd be great. I was going to open cans."

"Why don't I grill them?"

"You have charcoal?"

"Wouldn't buy salmon steaks without charcoal," Dunlap said.

"See you in an hour, then," I said.

* * *

For a last minute meal I surprised myself. I fried rice and steamed frozen vegetables, and baked half a dozen refrigerator rolls. While setting the table Dunlap and Bailey burst in. Bailey's tail wagged a mile a minute. "What's up with Bailey?"

"I bought a salmon steak for her, too. She supervised the grilling."

"They look grand," I said, inspecting the platter.

After the food was gone I put all the dishes in my dishwasher and we carried glasses of iced tea outside. I had a large flagstone patio which was covered with rows of tightly woven salt cedar limbs. The chairs were fashioned from stiff iron and painted to rust proof them from the weather, but they were exceptionally comfortable.

"This is a nice area," Dunlap remarked while sipping tea.

"If it weren't for my neighbors, I probably wouldn't stay," I said.

"You're kidding? This is a one-in-a-million property. Glad you've got a bunch of old ancients to keep you here."

I glanced up, my expression revealed my surprise. "Old ancients?"

"Yeah. I should've told you months ago. I know about your neighbors."

"How'd you figure it out?"

"The night Ben saved my life. I probably had about as bad a case of hypothermia as you can get and not be dead. There we were in the middle of a winter snow storm, Ronnie was locked in the trunk, I got shot, and the car was on fire. Everything happened so fast. Out of nowhere this little kid shows up. He wasn't even wearing shoes or a jacket. He raced right into the inferno around the car and tried to open the trunk. I thought I was dreaming, you know, people can't do stuff like that. Bailey was there, barking, running around, and I figured the dog was part of the dream. Thought I'd died, and all this stuff was surreal.

"Next thing I recall I was sitting on a log beside this little kid. There was a big pit full of hot wood coals and he said it was necessary to keep the fire hot so it wouldn't make smoke. Me and Ben were sitting there by the warm pit, but at the same time I could see myself covered in layers of blankets right there on the ground. I asked Ben if I was dead. He said he believed I was deciding whether I should go ahead and cross over. I asked him if he was dead and he said he died a long, long time ago. I asked him how he died. He said while gathering pinon nuts for his mother he was bitten by a rattlesnake. The snake's venom did not kill him, but an infection from the bite made him terribly ill and he crossed over."

"I never knew how Ben died," I said. The story Dunlap shared touched me deeply and for the first time I thought of Ben as a live child. I could imagine him gathering the best pinons to take home. I knew pinons were a popular source of high protein food for the ancients.

I also thought of Dunlap and how close he came to dying. I was amazed he hadn't frozen to death in spite of the warm pit fire, and I was even more impressed Ben had managed to prevent Dunlap's system from going septic. Blood poisoning killed Ben, and it almost killed Dunlap. "You are a lucky man," I said. "And you owe your life to that little kid."

"I do." Dunlap couldn't hold back his trademark smile.

"And you quickly realized Kopeki, Sam and Nakani were ancients, too?"

"That was an easy one. They always came and went in the same direction. I'd been back around there walking. Nothing there but old ruins."

"How about Mule and Rooster and the Happy Hens?"

"That was even easier. I haul livestock for a living. One mule and a bunch of chickens leave behind a lot of manure. No manure anywhere."

"You know, I never thought of it that way," I said.

"One thing I've always been curious about is the Haggis rabbit."

"Yeah?"

"I've got good vision now," Dunlap said, touching the rims of his new glasses. "So you won't be able to make up a story. What the hell is the Haggis rabbit?"

I stood up and headed for the house. "I'll get us some more iced tea," I said.

"Then you gonna tell me?"

"Sure," I said. My turn to grin.

While we sipped down our second tall glass of iced tea, I shared the lowdown about Haggis. I told him the whole story, including how he butchered Rudy.

"I don't understand how Rudy, who is a huge wolf, was a dog."

"Ben found him," I said.

"Found the wolf or the dog?"

"Dana and Ben decided I needed a pet. They took me to an animal shelter in Santa Fe. I'd looked over all the dogs, but I didn't connect with any of them. Ben suddenly appears from behind a locked door with a brown and black puppy. I discovered the puppy was about to be put to sleep. I fell in love with that puppy soon as I saw him. I called him Rude Rudy because he peed on my boot. Later that year Haggis killed him. Except he wasn't really a puppy. He'd been a Spirit Wolf the whole time. He came back as himself, a wolf, and he killed Haggis."

"That is wild, you gotta understand. If I hadn't experienced that day in the cave, sitting there with a little ghost kid, watching myself dying on the ground, I'd never believe any of this."

"Rudy isn't an ancient," I said.

"He isn't. What is he?"

"He is truly a Spirit," I said. "Nakani says he's always been here, will always be here. He is kind of magical. He can turn into other forms. He's been a puppy and a dog. He's also been a dove. His true nature seems to be as a big white wolf ... a lobo."

"Where is he from?"

"Heaven," I said.

"You serious?"

"He arrives from the sky, and he leaves by leaping into the sky and vanishing."

"You are flat out serious," Dunlap said. "This is wild stuff."

"Lot of things we don't understand in this universe," I shrugged. "I don't worry about trying to understand everything. There was a time in my life when I did try. Too many things don't have answers. It's a waste of time trying to figure them out. Besides, I don't think we need to understand."

The sun sets around nine o'clock during late June. We discussed my ancient neighbors and the special Spirit Wolf I called Rudy for another hour. Then we carried our glasses into the house and Dunlap thanked me for letting him sleep in Dana's adobe.

"You're always welcome to stay there," I said.

"Sure appreciate it," he said. "And I am more than grateful you let me park that big old ugly box trailer over there. If I'm gonna save enough to buy my own truck, I can't afford to pay storage to keep it somewhere else."

"One of these days you're going to have to deal with Ben, Mule, Rooster and the Happy Hens over that box. You hook it to a truck and take it out of here, they're going to be upset."

"I don't know why," he said. "It's just a big metal box."

I shrugged. "They think it's their cool clubhouse."

We both laughed, and Dunlap left, walking across the field toward the adobe.

CHAPTER SEVENTEEN

Rick bugged me to write a feature story covering the annual Fourth of July festivities in Mountainair, the small ranching village near where I used to live. The three hour drive required me to be on the road by seven o'clock in the morning. Parade began at ten, street vendors and art galleries touted their offerings all day, a children's rodeo began at noon, the best barbecue in the world was served at one, and the adult rodeo began around three. Truly an all day event.

"What're you doing back in town?" Grady, the local bar owner asked while we all sat on the sidewalk curb watching the parade. During my drinking days I rented the last stool at his counter. He'd see me sit there until I couldn't sit. I'm sure he'd enjoy having a dollar for all the times he picked me up off the floor and guided me to the doorway.

"Writing for Rick Bell again," I said.

"Yeah. I saw your piece about the crazy who's burning women to death."

"What'd you think?"

"Photographs were a good idea. He's looking for the same woman. Crazy, crazy. Where do nuts like that come from?"

"Glad you appreciate the photographs. I'm thinking they might save a life," I said. "Women who see themselves in that profile can change how they look."

"If they live in Central New Mexico. Won't help 'em anywhere else."

I nodded. The newspaper readership circulated around five counties in New Mexico. The parade finished up, I said goodbye to Grady, and proceeded to make my way around town. By five I had a dozen good photographs of events and several pages of notes for the feature piece.

* * *

Mule stood with his big head pressed against the large bay window. Rooster and the Happy Hens were lined up on pine tree limbs allowing them a clear view inside. Expecting to see Kopeki and Sam, I pushed the door wide. I didn't need to switch on the light. There was still a good hour before the sun set this summer evening, but what I saw nearly gave me a heart attack. Slowly I backed out the door and closed it. Perspiration beaded across my forehead. Probably from fear of being eaten alive. I stood there, wondering what to do, when Ben and Bailey raced up behind me.

"Did you see them?" Ben yelled excitedly.

"Where in the world did they come from? How did they get in my kitchen?"

"Dana-the-magic-White-Hawk brought them," Ben said proudly.

"Dana was here? My cousin was here today?"

"She said they drowned."

"Why didn't she wait for me?" My cousin returned and she didn't wait. I'd give a year of my life to simply sit and share a cup of coffee with her, listen to what she'd been doing since she crossed over. I'd never missed anyone as much as I missed my cousin. I couldn't believe she was here and she didn't wait to see me.

And, I'd really like to know why she left polar bears in the kitchen.

"They drowned," Ben repeated. "Dana said one day they'll all be gone. She helped them cross over. Then she brought them here."

"What am I supposed to do with them?" I asked.

"They are mine!" Ben squealed. He opened the kitchen door and raced inside with Bailey right behind. I watched from the safety of the doorway. Mule stood behind peering over my head. Ben dropped himself across the huge mother bear's back and two cubs began playing with him. The mother bear dropped her head on her feet. Bailey licked the bear's nose and she merely blinked. Cautiously I stepped across the threshold and inched toward the gigantic bear. She raised her head and watched me, seeming more curious than scary.

"You can pet her," Ben offered. He grabbed a handful of her snow white fur.

"Will she bite?"

Ben burst into laughter. "Why would she bite?"

The cubs ran toward me and I froze. They pawed at my feet, chewed on my sandals and sniffed my ankles before running back to jump on their mother's back.

"These are the best babies," Ben said. "You could pick them up."

"They have very sharp claws," I said.

"They are mine!" Ben squealed again, hugging the young cubs.

"Did Dana say when she'd be back?"

"She said she is not very far away, she will never be very far away and she touched the side of her head."

I remembered what Sam said about Larry Tawayesva. "Was she with Larry?"

Ben nodded while he played wrestle with the cubs. Sam was correct, Dana found her Tawayesva and they were together. I wished I'd known him. I felt overwhelmed for a moment with a grateful sense of calm. She crossed over and found the love of her life -- actually, the love of her after life, too.

"Well, now them's right fine lookin' animals," Sam said. Sam and Kopeki maneuvered past Mule, who blocked the open doorway. "Polar bears. I read about 'em in National Geographic. Always wanted to head up to Canada and see me some up close. Maybe not up too close," he said with a wink.

"Ben got some more pets." Kopeki grinned. His grinning reminded me of Dunlap and for a second I wondered why some people were always grinning.

"Mule?" Sam turned to look at Mule. "Whataya think of these new neighbors?"

"Phwshhh," Mule said. His sombrero tilted and I reached over to right it on his head.

"Bailey's right fond of 'em," Sam noted. Bailey sprawled beside the mother bear, both now had their heads on their front paws. "Missy," he turned to eye me. "Why are they in the kitchen?"

"Dana and Tawayesva brought them. This is where I found them when I got home tonight."

"She wanted you to see them," Ben said. "I'm gonna take them with me."

I stood in my yard with the most dumbfound expression I'd ever had. Sam and Kopeki walked behind Ben, who loped alongside the polar bears. Mule trailed after the men, and Rooster and the Happy Hens formed the caboose.

By now the night completed its descent across the hills and valleys, and within seconds the departing party vanished.

"Whoa." I couldn't think of anything else to say.

Bailey sat with me while we surveyed the darkness for a few minutes.

I was immediately relieved to know I'd never have to explain any of this to Dunlap.

I'd let Ben.

Polar bears in the kitchen.

Only Dana would think of that.

CHAPTER EIGHTEEN

The next day I coordinated my notes, matched three photographs with my final story, and sent it flying off to Rick. I had to admit, it was a really good feature piece and I was sure Rick would call immediately to tell me so. He did eventually phone that evening.

"Nice piece of fluff. I'll use one of the photographs."

"Oh no," I objected. "You'll use all the photographs. And it's not fluff. Hey. Did you even read it?"

"Sure I did."

"What's the primary theme?"

"Fourth of July."

"You didn't read it."

"Okay," Rick said. "I skimmed over. It's fine."

"The primary theme is the rodeo," I said. "The Mountainair Jubilee was created as filler fluff around the rodeo on July 4th. The photographs tie that theme together. If you don't use all of them, the story won't be as interesting."

"Okay."

"Okay and promise," I said.

"Okay and promise," Rick agreed.

I'd not seen any of my neighbors since the polar bear introduction and was about to walk toward the old ruins in search of them when I heard a car's tires crunching along my driveway.

Detective Shaw parked his generic black SUV. I met him at the edge of my patio.

"This isn't good news, is it?" I asked. His body language suggested his tone.

"No."

Shaw sat on a stool at the counter while I popped a couple cups of tea into the microwave. "You want sugar and lemon?" I asked.

"No, thanks."

I dropped a slice of lemon in my tea and joined him, seating myself across the counter.

"What can I say?" he began. "Budget cuts. We're understaffed. Everyone's understaffed these days. Salt Lake City is seriously understaffed."

"What happened?"

"We're off the record here, Myra."

"Off the record."

"The woman you told me about. She's dead."

"Oh my gosh! You're kidding? How'd she die?"

"Gunshot. One .22 caliber behind the ear. Execution style."

"When? Why? You said you'd have SLC keep an eye on her."

"Like I said," Shaw sighed and shrugged, "budget cuts."

"Mystery man should be your first suspect."

"And you're sure because?"

"She called me the night I got back from SLC. Told me she'd seen him."

"How's she know what he looked like?"

"I gave her Dunlap's description. She said she thinks she ran into him at the Winter Olympics in 2002."

"Ten years ago? No way she could remember that far back. I'm not buying that story. She may have known our perp."

"I don't even remember what I had for breakfast a few days ago, but I was giving her the benefit of the doubt."

"Whether her statement to you was accurate isn't as important right now as what it means," Shaw said. "A connection puts that investigation into Fed territory and opens up their methods of discovery. Most important, their budget is bigger than ours."

"Can't believe this. My first thinking was the mystery man killed her. But the gun, that's … wait a minute. He shot Dunlap. Bullet fragment and shell casings are here. On my property."

"You got the bullet?"

"I've got the bullet," I said. "Casings are still out there where the car burned."

"You have some small plastic bags?"

I reached beneath the counter and pulled out a box of sandwich bags. "Like this?"

"Like that."

"Anything else?"

"You got a digital camera?"

"Yes."

"Get it."

I crossed the kitchen and pulled my camera from my handbag.

"Let's go," Shaw said.

We hiked first to the cave where Ben kept Dunlap alive. The bullet fragment was in the dirt near the fire pit. Shaw scooped it into a baggy using the tip of his writing pen.

"Wish you'd told me about this," he said, in reference to the bullet fragment.

"I told you Dunlap was shot. You never said anything about the bullet fragment."

"My failure," he said. "No excuses. That was bad investigation."

We continued on from the cave to the burn site and began searching slowly, carefully.

"If you find something, don't touch it," Shaw said.

We searched for almost an hour and found nothing. "You said the perp never returned to the scene of the crime," Shaw said. "Could you be mistaken?"

I considered all my neighbors. If the killer came back here, they'd know. "I'm sure no one's been here," I said.

"Nothing here." Shaw's tone expressed disappointment.

"Wait a minute," I said. "Snow. The place was covered in several feet of snow. The lower layers would have been hard packed. When snow melts it picks up what's beneath and carries those objects."

We both fell to our knees again and carefully searched the ground, inching further from the site. I was ready to give up.

"Got one!" Shaw yelled. "Bring your camera. We want a photograph before I move it."

"I've got one, too," I said, spotting the shiny oblong object. I photographed them. Shaw picked them up with his pen, dropped each one into a separate plastic bag, zipped the bags shut, dropped them into his pocket.

"Good work," he said.

"You're welcome. What're you gonna do with these?"

"We match bullet fragments and shell casings to the same gun, we've got a serial killer with a personal connection to his most recent vic."

Shaw pulled out his cell phone.

"Cell phones don't work out here," I said.

"They don't? You mind if I go back and use your land line?"

Shaw called his office in Santa Fe. From his end of the conversation I could tell, budget or lack of a budget, things were getting ready to get busy.

"When you going to let me write about this?" I asked.

"Hopefully, soon," Shaw said. "Until I say, I've got your word this is all off the record, and you don't know anything about what's in these baggies."

"I wrote about the similarities," I said.

"I read it. Not sure if it was a good idea to publish those photographs."

"If a photo has already been published in a newspaper, we can use it with permission from the first publication. Those photos were second time prints."

"For some reason he hasn't returned to this crime scene," Shaw said. "We never made the location public, so he might have forgotten how to get here."

"Around the time of the accident we had a whiteout," I said. Whiteouts are snow storms which are so thick, there is no visibility. You cannot see any distance beyond your windshield. What you do see is a white blanket of snow.

"That explains why he never came back," Shaw said. "He wasn't driving. Dunlap was driving, and the killer wouldn't have any references."

"Let me get you another cup of tea," I said, noticing Shaw's cup was empty.

"No, thanks. I need to get back to town."

"Humor me," I said. "I spend more than ninety percent of my time alone. Your news isn't good, and this meeting isn't entertaining, but I enjoy the company. I'm going to have another cup, and so are you."

* * *

I had an assortment of pottery to deliver in Old Town the following day. When I returned home there were no phone calls, but Dunlap's box trailer was full of characters. Ben was nowhere to be found. His polar bears, Mule and Bailey were napping inside the trailer. July heat is suppressive, even in the Northern New Mexico Rocky Mountain range. I guessed the temperature inside that metal box had to be around one hundred. Good thing these polar bears didn't care about temperature anymore.

I left the menagerie to get on with their summer nap, returned to my house and watched the clock hoping my phone would ring.

Three days later it rang.

"Detective Shaw here."

"What can you tell me?"

"Off the record, Myra. This is for your ears only until I say otherwise."

"My ears are the only ones listening."

"It's the same gun. Feds sent the bullets and casings off to their lab. Firing pin left imprints which matched for all bullet fragments. Casings all have the same scratch and dent which indicates the gun clip is defective."

"Any DNA?

"Better than that. One of the casings from SLC had a partial print. We've got a name and feds have a warrant"

"Who is he?"

"Roscoe Flannery."

"Where does he live?"

"Salt Lake City. He works for the Utah Division of Motor Vehicles."

"DNA on the cigarettes?"

"All matches," Shaw said.

"And he's been arrested?"

"He had a lot of vacation time and he took it. We lost his trail."

"How could that happen?"

"It happens."

"What now?" I asked.

"Whataya mean, what now? We'll catch him."

"Any idea ... "

"No more questions," Shaw said. "And by the way, soon as I hang up, everything you know is still off the record."

"Until when?"

"Until he's arrested." The familiar sound of a closed buzzing line ensued.

Chapter Nineteen

*P*sychopath serial killer working for the Utah Division of Motor Vehicles.
If Shaw let me write about what I knew, that would be my head-line. I guessed as to the *how* part, but I believe I moved beyond luke warm to pssssssss hot. Roscoe Flannery found his targets using state computer networks.

Were there search categories?

Of course. There had to be. I imagined he randomly selected a city he could easily fly into and out of, where he'd be one more anonymous face. He must've input his criteria and later studied the results.

Living in Salt Lake City explained away some of what I knew about him. He was a hiker and an outdoors man possessing hefty survival skills which answered my question as to how he always fled the crime scene without a car regardless the weather conditions. He dressed for the weather, he was athletic, and he knew how to travel great distance on foot.

Still didn't explain how he knew his targets would be athletic. My driver's license did not indicate marital status, either, and I assumed this would be consistent in all states, which also meant he had no idea who would or would not wear a wedding ring.

I knew the police investigations would uncover Flannery's connection with the woman he'd shot. I wondered why she bothered to call me and make something up. Unless, of course, she wanted attention on Flannery, even if it meant exposing herself.

Exposing herself to what? Danger? Redundant now.

Who was he to her?

Who was she to him?

Roscoe Flannery murdered the same woman over and over again. He relentlessly hunted her down. Didn't matter if she was seventeen or fifty. Didn't matter if her name was Agatha or Zoë. In his mind they were all the same woman.

He wanted that woman gone.

Was that why he burned them? Because he really wanted them to disappear?

Up in smoke?

Dust in the wind?

I read all the autopsy reports Rick could come up with and, with the exception of Veronica North, they were either suffocated or strangled. They died before their fiery farewell.

Back to North. We'd never know unless Flannery told us, yet my belief was she became the worst offender of all the targets. North was the impostor. He would perceive she only pretended to be that other woman and he didn't discover her chicanery until Dunlap showed up in the parking lot that night. He punished her for that deception by allowing her to suffer.

Why car trunks?

Symbolic coffins?

Did he also see this?

Is that why he put them in the trunk?

Was he ceremoniously burying them? After all, they were dead. He didn't have to lock them in the trunk to keep them from escaping.

Could SLC's new homicide be that woman, the one he kept eliminating?

My hand was busy making notes and my thoughts were even busier making these things up while I went along. I had no idea what the outcome of all Flannery's killings would be. Seemed like there ought to be one.

I could feel my heart rate increasing and my anxiety rising. I knew putting all these thoughts in my head were the cause of the uncomfortable manifestations. Distraction is what I needed.

After checking the oil and fuel levels in my weed cutter, I started it up and began cutting grass and weeds. Working from my house moving out approximately fifty feet, I cleaned this distance for the full area all around my home and porches. Dana taught me to do this because we had clumps of heavily forested property. She called this a firebreak. Although I always wondered how much a fifty foot distance would matter if fire erupted on these densely treed hills.

The yard work took several hours, including another hour to rake up the cuttings, load these into the old GMC and haul all the organic debris to a nearby arroyo where I dumped it. First good rain would mulch the entire mess.

One good hot shower and fresh clean clothes put me back in a thinking mood. I was about to pull out my notes when Dunlap's empty livestock hauler pulled up across the field. He parked it next to his box trailer. I set my iced tea down and strolled over to say hello.

"You delivered another load of mother cows in New Mexico," I said.

"No," Dunlap grimaced. "I'm picking up the herd I delivered in Ramah a month ago."

"Why?"

"They didn't pay for them," Dunlap said.

"Not your fault."

"I accepted their check when I unloaded them."

"Is that what you're supposed to do?"

"I'm supposed to get a cashier's check or a money order," Dunlap said. "They paid with a company check, and it wasn't any good."

"Let's go over to my house," I said. "I'll pour you some tea. You hungry?"

"I picked up more of them salmon steaks when I came through Santa Fe. Got two big potatoes, too." Dunlap's cheer returned. He was grinning.

"Well," I said. "I hope you're staying over this evening. Dana's house is clean, just like you always leave it."

"I can do that. The herd's been delivered to the fair grounds in Albuquerque, and that's where I pick 'em up tomorrow morning. My boss turned the bad check over to the district attorney in Texas and the local law enforcement here confiscated the cows."

While we walked to my house Dunlap lost his grin again. "I almost got fired."

"I'm surprised your boss leaves it to the driver to collect the money."

"Won't make much difference," Dunlap said. "In a few months I'll have saved about enough. I'm gonna start looking for my own truck. I can make five hundred dollars for hauling frozen food short distances. After buying fuel and paying my own taxes, I'll still make good money. One of these days I'll even get me a house. I never had a real home. You lettin' me stay at your cousin's house, sure opens my eyes. Nothing like having your own place."

"Sit out here where it's shady," I said when we reached my porch. "I'll get the tea."

Within a few minutes we were talking about how nice my place showed in the middle of a hot parched summer. "It doesn't look like this without a lot of effort. I cut all this grass today," I said, waving my hands to take in the wide circumference. "Hours of labor, but at least I don't have to do it more than three or four times a year." I inhaled deeply. Fresh cut grass has an intoxicating smell.

"Where's Bailey?" Dunlap jumped the subject. Probably because he didn't want me handing him the weed cutters next time he dropped in.

"With the neighbors. By the way, we got some new ones."

"Real neighbors?"

"Ben can introduce you." My turn to grin.

A few hours later that evening we sat on the same porch enjoying a wonderful repast. Dunlap had a touch for grilled salmon. After cooking the large baking potatoes, I cut them lengthwise, carefully scooped the cooked potato away from the peels, mashed the potato with diced onion, parsley, butter, and lemon zest, then refilled the potato skins with my new potato treat. A dollop of sour cream topped these off, and they were delicious alongside the salmon.

"We ought make a bunch of these and sell 'em" Dunlap commented on my potato dish.

"Sure," I said. "We could package them and use your frozen food box trailer. What should we ask? Five dollars for a serving for two?"

"Five dollars for two," he agreed with a nod.

"What should we call them?"

"Potato boats," Dunlap said.

"Potato boats it is."

"Bark, barka." Bailey announced herself while racing across the porch to her water dish.

"Salmon for you, too." Dunlap got up from his chair and fetched the piece he'd cooked for her. She swallowed it without chewing. "Makes you wonder why I bother," he said.

"She eats like that to let you know how much she enjoys the good fish."

"She doesn't even take time to savor the flavor."

"You're right. She doesn't. Next time get her a rawhide chew. Takes her a couple minutes to devour those."

That evening we sat on the porch talking about nonsense, like marketing potato boats from a refrigerated truck. The night sky filled with constellations, which we pretended we knew, and Mule showed up to listen.

"Sombrero still looks brand new," Dunlap noted.

"I notice that, too. Guess ghost mules don't soil their attire." I shrugged at the curious thought.

"He doesn't smell bad, you know," Dunlap said.

I laughed. "Yeah. I know that, too. I always wondered if you'd figure there was something odd about a mule with no odor."

Mule stood nearby taking in everything we said. Occasionally he nodded his big head, and once I had to get up to center the sombrero when it nearly fell off over his ears.

Dunlap retired around midnight. I loaded dishes into my dishwasher before going to bed.

Early the next morning I heard yelling and exclamations which would blush a sailor. I ran across the field and saw the back of Dunlap's box trailer wide open.

"Bears!" It was all Dunlap could say.

I glanced around. Ben, Bailey and Mule were no where to be seen. I walked over and peered inside.

"Polar bears," I corrected him.

CHAPTER TWENTY

"Roscoe Flannery had a history of stalking the vic he shot in Salt Lake City." Detective Shaw spoke from his office telephone.

"You're serious? I can believe stalking, but a real police record?"

"Couple years before the 2002 Winter Olympics she filed complaints. He was warned but never charged."

"And she kept this a secret because?"

"Good question. Not one we'll get answers to, I'm sure."

"She fooled me," I said. "She gave me a story about him coming on to her during one of the events. Said he left her alone when her husband showed up."

"Can't rule out she wasn't telling the truth about that segment."

"She could have included the stalker complaints."

"You wanted a connection," Shaw said. "That's it."

"She's been investigated that far back?"

"Routine, considering who shot her."

"Okay," I said. "When can I publish my story?"

"Not yet."

"You going to tell me why?"

"Flannery has no idea we're on to him."

"And does anyone have any idea where he is?"

"Feds think he's here."

"Santa Fe?"

"New Mexico. I agree. He thinks he needs to find Dunlap. In his twisted mind, he might see Dunlap as the only way these roads turn around and head right back to him."

My heart rate increased and I began to feel physically horrible. "He'll cruise all the highways out of Santa Fe," I said, "trying to recall this route. He may have gotten a ride. That person must've given him a clue where he was at. Eventually, Flannery could end up here."

"We'll notify County, make sure they send cruisers your direction a couple times every twenty four hours."

"That makes me feel peachy," I said, using the most sarcastic tone I could muster.

"You could find somewhere else to live. At least until he's cuffed."

I hung up on Shaw and immediately checked all my windows and doors. When cleaning out Dana's house I'd discovered what I guessed to have once been Tawayesva's hand gun, an M9 Beretta. They are similar to a Glock 9 mm in size, weight, and general destruction of whatever ends up on the receiving side of the cartridge. Nine millimeter rounds are slow and lose accuracy after about 55 yards, which means timing and aim are equally important. Besides that minor glitch, a better self defense weapon is difficult to find. I fetched gun and holster and fastened them to my belt.

I decided to ride Mule around my property, and to then head out across neighbor properties which had access to the highway. No way to secure wilderness homes, but I needed an idea regarding the layout of tree thickets, caves, rock formations, old ruin sites, anywhere Flannery might hole up and hide.

Soon as Mule spotted me dragging his saddle from my storage shed he was right in my face. "You think you need your sombrero?" I asked, knowing he would not appreciate me removing this prize possession. Leaving his hat in place I slid the bridle muzzle over his nose, heaved the saddle over the saddle blanket, and cinched it down tight.

Within minutes we traveled south, down the lengthy driveway, then across the paved road. All the properties were well fenced along the highways. New Mexico has old rancher's rules which require this. Once it'd been a safety factor protecting open range livestock from meeting with untimely death-by-vehicle-collision accidents. Now it was simply the law, which meant we had to follow fence lines until there were unlocked gates. Most properties were entered across cattle guards, but State law also required gates in the fencing adjacent to all cattle guards. Again, these were rules to protect livestock. A person would never want to ride a horse across a cattle guard, no more than they'd send cattle over these. The result would likely be broken legs.

August is typically hot, arid and dusty in New Mexico. This day was no exception. I emptied my canteen of water within the first two hours and had to back track home to refill. I left Mule in the yard while I splashed water across my face, neck and arms. This helped removed dirt from my pores thus cooling me off.

"You going on a trail ride?" Sam's voice asked from my open kitchen doorway.

"I'm researching," I said. I didn't know how much to fill him in, or how much he'd be interested in knowing.

"Researching your perimeters?" Sam asked.

"The man who burned Veronica North to death last November is now on the run."

"You figurin' he's a runnin' this way?" Sam walked across the kitchen and sat on one of the counter stools. His expression told me he did want to know what was going on, or going down. I filled him in, gave him all the information I knew was factual. I omitted my suspicions and opinions. This was something I learned from Dana. When an issue was important, all the importance faded if the issue became clouded and fuzzy due to suspicions and opinions.

"Just the facts, m'am," Dana liked to remind me. Just the facts is what I shared. Sam listened carefully with his full attention, even though my story took over an hour to explain. About the time I was finishing, Kopeki arrived.

"A very good day for a cup of coffee," Kopeki said with his huge toothless grin.

"Temperature is in the upper nineties," I winked at Sam, then fetched the coffee grounds and filtered water. Sam and Kopeki did not experience heat of summer, nor cold of winter. Just then I remembered Mule, who was on the porch waiting for me, still wearing his saddle. "Enjoy your coffee," I said. "I need to finish what I started."

"You be careful, Missy," Sam cautioned. "That wolf of your'n might know you could use back-up these days, but then, he might not. We'll keep an eye around this situation. Don't know what we can do to help. But we'll do the best we can."

"Thanks, Sam," I said. "I need all the help I can get, from wherever it arrives."

* * *

Our efforts netted a bit of satisfaction. The geography on this side of the road was about as rough and humanly uninhabitable as one could imagine. Massive rocks climbed toward the sky on north facing sides, suddenly dropping onto steep jagged cliffs toward each south side. These formations always indicated where mountains and hills grew out of the earth's surface during earthquakes and volcano eruptions. New Mexico was known for having a volatile history of occurrences like this in days long past.

Where soil allowed for deep roots, thick groves of pinon, cedar and ponderosa pine populated the terrain. No caves, no sources of water, nothing which would provide a person with comfortable security, even for a few hours. The ground surface was equally hostile. Without a stable durable type of boot, this land could destroy foot protection within one hour. If a person wore regular athlete's shoes they'd be in trouble. The terra firma would shred them.

Twice we encountered rattlesnakes. Both snakes were from the timber rattler group, huge and deadly venomous reptiles. One bite from them in this wilderness region more than likely meant death for their ill-fated victim. I thought about young Ben. Such had been the end of his childhood, and his life, hundreds of years earlier. And I considered Flannery. Utah had its share of snakes. Flannery would know the hazards of this land. He was an outdoors man, a skilled hiker, a survivalist of sorts.

I'd never trespassed on so many people's private property all in one day, but these were wide open high country ranges. Most being old ranches that hadn't seen livestock in at least a couple dozen years according to the absence of any trace of animal waste or carcass.

At sundown we crossed back over the highway onto my property, and from the driveway entry we headed north, west, and eventually east toward the houses. There were no signs of an intruder. Plenty of wildlife tracks and droppings, but mortal intrusion? Zero.

New Mexico's soil contains too much clay content. Tire tracks and foot prints can remain a year or longer unless rain, snow and wind disturb them, which is difficult for most to comprehend. Having worked this soil into clay pottery, pots which could last for hundreds of years, I did comprehend.

Before removing Mule's tack, I ran to the house and let Bailey out. She was furious at not being allowed to travel with us on this day. Yet, Bailey was extremely elderly, and although I knew she ran the hills with Ben and Mule, and sometimes Rudy, their adventures always took place during cooler hours. Those were exercise opportunities which kept her healthy. At her age she might have a heat stroke or cardiac failure.

"I'm sorry old girl," I apologized. Bailey eyed me with disfavor before sniffing the saddle with the same intensity one might read a history book. The saddle revealed where we'd been, those areas she'd been denied to accompany us this day.

"Growl!" Bailey exclaimed, then disappeared in the direction of the old ruins. There she'd find a friendly face who'd listen to her grievances.

I pulled my pistol from the holster and released the safety before checking Dana's adobe, the ceramic studio, the storage shed, both vehicles, and my house. I didn't bother much with Dunlap's box trailer because it locked from the outside making this an inconvenient hiding place. When I felt sure all was clear I slipped the Beretta safety back in place and took a shower, washing off at least five pounds of New Mexico dirt. There are few ways to collect more soil on ones person than horseback riding, especially during the dry summer months.

That evening I pulled out all my research and interview notes, spread them on my kitchen work counter, then began sorting them. The conviction that Flannery's shooting vic was the key tugged at me. He killed her because he knew this, as well.

Someone in her history must know how these two people knew each other. I had her work history records and her sister's address. No need to stress it. I pulled my suitcase from the closet and packed for three days. Bailey and I were going back to SLC in the morning.

CHAPTER TWENTY-ONE

"My name is Myra Whitehawk," I spoke through the screen door. "I'm a newspaper reporter. I hope you will give me a few minutes of your time."

The small sixtyish woman opened the screen. "Come on in. I don't have to ask you why you're here. You want to know about Anne."

Anne was the shooting vic's name. I'd all but tried to not use her name. When I thought of the woman, I thought in terms of victim. Made me feel less guilty. I called Shaw, alerted him to the danger I believed she was in, and no one did anything. The cops were comfortable using budget as their excuse. We could all pretend she was killed because she didn't give up her story, the part where she knew Flannery. Facts remained, she died because everyone involved in Flannery's case let her down. He'd been getting away with murder for a decade that we knew of, so he assumed killing her would be just another crime without punishment.

"Yes, m'am," I said, crossing over her threshold and surveying the small tidy house.

"We worked together at an old drugstore downtown," the woman continued. She was eager to talk and I hadn't even sat down. I reached in my handbag, pulled out my recorder and switched it to *on*.

"Have a seat anywhere that's not taken," she said.

Three big fat cats sprawled about on two chairs and a love seat. She picked up one of the chair squatters and plopped it in her lap. I followed her lead and picked up the love seat napper and plopped it on one side of the sofa.

"Do the police think it was her ex-husband that shot her?" the woman asked.

"I don't know," I coached. "Why? Do you think he had a motive?"

"Well," she hesitated. "They always think it's the husband, you know. He's long gone. Left Utah years ago. But Anne had that boyfriend. He was the creepiest weirdo I ever met. Don't know why she cheated on her husband with that weirdo. Wrecked her marriage."

"Could you tell me more about the boyfriend?"

"What do you want to know about him? I only saw him a few times. When he came by the store to check up on Anne."

"Tell me anything you remember."

"He was blond. Had some kinda weirdo hair style. Punky style. He was Anne's age. I think he had a teenager's hair style, though. That's odd, you know. Punky, you know. Weirdo. What the heck did she see in him?"

"Was he athletic?"

"You know them wannebe-a-sports-star kind?"

I nodded.

"He came in wearing those weirdo outfits. Those kinda clothes that look like somebody painted them on. And he had earrings. I wondered if he was a homosexual, you know what I mean. What kinda man wears earrings?"

"You recall his name?"

"I couldn't forget that creeps name if I wanted to," she said. "Weirdo name. Roscoe. I thought he made that up. Who names their kid Roscoe? That's a dog's name."

Our conversation continued two pieces of coffee cake and four cups of tea later. Her information was sparse but essential. I now had a good idea why Anne didn't tell the truth about Flannery. She had an affair with him and when it looked like it was affecting her marriage, she dumped him. That was the year of the 2002 Winter Olympics. She probably did see Roscoe at the event. Her story was likely true about him stalking her then vanishing when her husband showed up. Unfortunately she left out the affair piece and it cost a life: her own.

Anne's sister moved to Alaska so I decided that interview wouldn't be a face to face, but I had her new phone numbers, which I'd use. I did find several more early coworkers who knew Anne during the affair era, but none had met Flannery, nor did they know anything about him.

Two days in Salt Lake City and I had as much as I was getting. After loading Bailey, I drove half the night until we reached home. First thing I saw was the blinking message indicator. Five messages from Detective Shaw and two from Rick Bell. I didn't listen to them. I was too exhausted. If the news was bad, I'd rather hear it in the morning. I showered and went to bed.

Around seven the next day I awoke after less than four hours of rest. Grumbling and cursing I crawled from bed and saw Shaw's SUV pulling into my yard. I climbed into jeans and a t-shirt and met him at my kitchen door.

"I called you six times yesterday." His tone expressed disquietude.

"Five," I corrected. "I was in Salt Lake City."

"What were you doing there?"

"Looking for a connection between the victim he shot and himself."

"They were in high school together," Shaw said, seating himself at the dining room table. "You gonna make some coffee?"

"I don't have decaf."

"Coffee. Please."

"Anyone ever tell you you're a bit bossy in the morning?" I asked.

"Ex-wife said that all the time."

"She was right."

"I'd sure like to see that coffee getting made," Shaw said.

I pulled my decanter, filters, and a couple of coffee cups from cabinets and started the brew. "Makes sense," I said, "about high school. Furthest back I could find a link was 2002. He's killed before that time, so that didn't make sense. You want eggs and toast?"

"No food," Shaw said.

I began scrambling eggs and buttering bread. I slipped four slices of bread into the toaster oven. When all was ready, I set a plate in front of Shaw and he began eating. Soon as the coffee finished, I handed him a cup. "Cowboy style?" I asked.

"Is there any other style? Sugar and cream ruin the taste."

I poured myself one, cowboy style, and sat across the table.

"Surprised to find high school records that many years ago," Shaw said. "They didn't put everything on computers in the eighties. We had to dig up people with good memories. But this is pretty interesting, and I know you'll agree. When the vic was in ninth grade, Flannery was a senior. He never actually talked to the vic ... "

"Anne," I interrupted.

Shaw paused and flashed a perturbed look at me. "Like I was saying, he never met her. They shared P.E. That's the old physical education hour. Girls were on one side of the gym, boys on the other. He develops a crush on our vic. Begins writing her letters. He never sends them. One of his teachers discovers some of the letters. The content alarms the teacher, who shares them with the principal. Flannery is suspended for a week, told to stop the letter writing. He's a smart kid. Good grades. He stops doing his homework and flunks his senior year. A few months into the vic's sophomore year, Flannery buys her a ring. He starts up with the letters again. Mind, he's never met the vic, never talked to her. She has no idea she's being stalked all through ninth grade, right into tenth grade. One of the hall duty teachers starts noticing Flannery's odd behaviors in his attention to the vic and that teacher alerts the principal. The principal tells that teacher about the previous trouble. Flannery gets transferred to another high school. Every one thinks it's the end of the story."

"What did the letters say?" I asked.

"Not exactly sure," Shaw said. "The teacher who recalls all this is now a retired counselor. She was the one with hall duty. She said when she told the principal she'd noticed Flannery following the vic every day, always watching her, the principal showed her a file with the letters from the previous incident. The teacher said the letters expressed a relationship, as if they were an old married couple. Flannery developed an attraction, then he conjured up an entire lover's relationship which never happened. Anne probably didn't even know who this guy was, and if she'd ever known what he'd been up to in high school, she'd have run first time she saw him many years later, around early 2000."

"That is bizarre."

"Stalkers tend to progress through three stages," Shaw continued. "First stage is attraction. Flannery was attracted to the vic first time he saw her when she was a freshman in high school. He began following her, writing letters, even bought a ring for her. That was the obsession stage. Their relation was his fantasy and he fed it every time he wrote one of those letters. He was moving beyond obsession when he bought the ring. Final stage of stalking is destruction. At some point in his life, probably a long time before she knew he existed, he decided to destroy her one piece at a time. Each time he killed one of her look-alikes, he was destroying another piece of her. He could not stop killing the look-alikes because with each new murder, he realized she was still haunting him."

"I realized that, too. The part where he was killing Anne, over and over again."

Shaw sighed heavily and offered his empty cup. I poured him another shot of brew.

"Through the years I've been a street cop," he said, "and a detective, and you cannot even imagine -- you don't want to imagine -- the stuff I've seen. You'd never sleep if you knew what some people are capable of doing to other people."

"You forget, I knew Haggis up close and personal. But I don't think you called five times yesterday to tell me Flannery stalked Anne since high school."

"He's been using stolen identities every time he travels, rents cars, checks into motels. His job made it easy since all the information anyone ever needs to steal someone else's identity has been at his fingertips."

"Utah Division of Motor Vehicles. Why didn't you guys figure that one out sooner?"

"He's a supervisor in the branch he works at. I'd guess if anyone suspected one of the employees was pilfering through the state's files, stealing people's private information, Flannery was in the best position to sabotage those suspicions."

"Who is he pretending to be right now?" I asked.

"We don't know."

"Which means he has a good disguise."

"That's right." Shaw handed me his empty cup.

"You remember, this is buzz coffee," I said.

"I remember."

I poured up what remained in the pot and handed him his third cup.

"Flannery is about as dangerous as they get," Shaw said. "If he shows up out here, dial 911 and get inside. Arm yourself. And wait for the sheriff's deputies."

"I'll do that," I said, meaning I'd arm myself.

Shaw drained his cup and stood. "You've got my number, too."

"Got all your numbers," I said.

Shaw walked out onto the porch. Bailey chased the Haggis rabbit off in the distance. I held my breath and hoped she did not chase it this direction.

"There's that goddamn deformed rabbit," Shaw said. "Get me your rifle. I'm gonna shoot that damn thing and put it out of its misery."

I hesitated, then thought, what the heck. I crossed the kitchen and retrieved my long range .22 rifle.

"Bailey!" I called out. "Here, girl!"

Bailey ran across the field toward me. When she was on my patio Shaw pulled the trigger and the Haggis rabbit fell in its tracks.

"Don't know why you didn't shoot that thing." Shaw made a face and shook his head.

"You let me know if anyone figures out what Flannery is driving, or where he's staying," I said while walking to Shaw's SUV.

"Will do." He crawled in and drove away.

Within a few minutes I glanced toward the Haggis rabbit. It was up and running off in the direction of the old ruins.

Doomed.

Cursed.

Haggis would not be freed from his punishment by a bullet.

Haggis would not be free until the Spirit Wolf decided.

CHAPTER TWENTY-TWO

I waited until the next day to think about my next move. I rose early and took my cup of tea out onto my patio. Who would I call first? Probably needed to return Rick's calls. And I wanted to talk with Anne's sister. Wasn't sure what she could provide me, but anything she knew would be information for the piece I had in mind.

While I dialed her number in Alaska I anticipated whether she'd even talk to me.

"How may I direct your call?" the voice asked.

"Hello," I paused. Sounded like a business, not a residence. "My name is Myra Whitehawk. I am a newspaper reporter. I'm looking for ... "

"Anne's sister?" the voice interrupted.

"That's correct."

"Speaking. I'm at work. I can't tie this line up for more than a few minutes."

"Do you have another phone ... "

"No, I do not." She cut me off.

"I'll get right to the point. Do you have any knowledge of a man ... "

"Roscoe Flannery," she interrupted again.

"You knew him?"

"Biggest freak I ever met. What my sister saw in him I will never know. I told the cops he was the one who shot her."

"Why would you think this?"

"Because he threatened her. I don't know how often. I do know she moved half a dozen times, kept unlisted phone numbers, he always found her. He works at that freaking vehicle registration place. He could find her phone number and address anytime he wanted it. Total freak. I knew he was gonna hurt her one of these days. He killed her, didn't he?"

"I'm not a cop," I said, my tone apologetic. "I just write stories for newspapers."

"So why were you wanting to know about Roscoe?"

"He looks like a primary suspect to me."

"Yeah, you and me can agree on that. Too bad the cops have been ignorant. It's their fault she's dead. Cops told her so many times they couldn't arrest him until he actually did something. Well, he did something. And they still haven't arrested him."

"How well did you know him?"

"Other than knowing he was a total freak, I didn't know him. Met him not more than two or three times."

"Where did you know him?"

"You mean how did I meet him? Not formally, if that's what you mean. I didn't know Anne had an affair with him. Years later she was scared, came over to my house middle of the night. That's when I first heard about him. He found out where she was living and he tried to break in while she was sleeping. She got out the back door, managed to get a ride to my place, wearing her pajamas. Can you believe that? She called the cops from my place and guess what they did? Nothing. They said there were no eye witnesses. Freaking unbelievable."

"I have to agree, that is freaking unbelievable. So, you are saying Roscoe Flannery stalked her for how many years -- that you know of?"

"About eight or ten."

"Did you ... "

"My supervisor is walking this direction. Gotta go."

The sound of a dead line indicated our interview ended. That was okay. I now had more of a picture around Anne's relationship with Flannery. After he finally insinuated himself into Anne's life, he stalked and he terrorized her. When her coworker was murdered and cremated in her own car, Anne suspected him. He'd given her years of reason to do just that.

She'd never be able to tell me, or the cops. But then, the cops practically sanctioned Flannery's terrorist behavior toward her all those years. Whatever she knew or suspected, they'd be the last place she'd look for help.

All the women's deaths were unnecessary tragedies, yet this one haunted me. Not because Flannery launched his serial career with obsessions around a young unsuspecting high school freshman, but because her death was the one that could have been prevented.

I dialed Shaw's number and told him what I planned on doing.

The lengthy pause on his end suggested displeasure. Eventually he responded. "Nothing there compromises this case."

"I need some of the names of the people you told me about."

"Thought I gave them to you."

"You gave me their positions. Not names."

Shaw grudgingly provided the information. I kept my word, and would continue to do so regarding all the *off the record* material, but he felt backed into a corner and I knew it.

"Send me a copy of the published story," he said.

"Paper's on every newsstand in Santa Fe," I said. "But I'll fax you a copy before it goes into print."

Shaw hung up and I sat for a few moments, allowed my decision to settle.

Carrying my laptop out onto the porch, I settled into a chair with its back near the kitchen wall and began the story. Shaw was not happy but he couldn't object because it would not include any of the *for my ears only* information.

When I finished the piece a few hours later I hit the *send* button and let it fly to Rick.

Late that afternoon my phone rang.

"You like?" I asked the caller.

"This is good," Rick sounded quite pleased. "And you learned all this when?"

"I gathered quite a bit from the first time I went to Salt Lake City," I said. "I knew stuff was missing, so I drove back over there a few days ago. Talked to people she'd known all the way back to the first job she had after high school."

"Myra," Rick said. I'd known Rick Bell long enough to understand when he made a complete sentence using only my name, he was politely asking how much I knew beyond the story I'd written.

"It's all going to tie together," I said.

"She worked with one of the serial killer's victims. Serial killer struck twice in New Mexico. Now she's dead, but no one's making the connection. I know you are doing just that. When are you going to fill me in with the rest of the details?"

"I'd tell you now, but I don't trust telephones."

"I'll drive up there," Rick said.

"You coming now?"

"Be there by seven."

"Bring dinner."

"What do you want?"

"Something fried and full of calories."

"I can do that," Rick said, hanging up.

I hadn't cleaned my house in a week. After loading my dishwasher I ran the vacuum, dusted all the furniture tops, cleaned the guest bathroom, and draped fresh towels across the racks.

"Myra!" Ben called from my kitchen.

I glanced at the clock. Rick would not arrive for another hour. "Where are your polar bears?" I asked.

"In the club house," Ben grinned. "We're pretending it's snowing."

The club house was Dunlap's box trailer. "Is Bailey there with you?"

"Yes."

"And the Haggis rabbit?"

"No. The baby bears keep eating it."

"Oh? Okay. Well, listen. Rick Bell is driving up for dinner. He'll be here soon. Do you think you could keep the polar bears busy, maybe in the old ruins?"

"Okay," Ben said. Always agreeable. Always cheerful.

"And before you leave, could you send Bailey home?"

"Okay. Can we have some candles?"

"Yes," I said, removing a package of all purpose candles from a drawer near the sink. "What are you going to use them for?"

"We're going to the cave. We just want some candles." With that Ben disappeared. A few minutes later Bailey was at the kitchen door wanting inside. She ignored me and ran to her cushion in the den.

"Ben told you I wouldn't let you play with them after dark, didn't he?" I asked the perturbed dog.

Bailey turned her back to me and went to sleep. I could not make her understand what Haggis had done to Rudy. I would not take a chance Flannery might show up and do harm to this old dog who, unlike Rudy, could not reappear as a wolf seeking vengeance. I had not seen Mule or Rooster and the Happy Hens. I assumed they were all with Ben and his polar bears, heading for the cave where Ben had kept Dunlap alive.

"You got something cold to drink?" Rick asked, walking into my kitchen without knocking.

"I've got lemonade and tea," I said.

"Perfect."

"Which one?"

"Pour some tea on top of my lemonade," he said. He placed a large delicious smelling sack on the counter.

"We need plates?"

"I wouldn't mind eating off a plate," he said.

I set plates, iced drinks and ketchup on the table. Rick removed two huge green chili cheeseburgers from the sack and put one on each plate. He then pulled out two large bags of fries and placed these on the plates. We both sat down and began eating.

"These are great," I said. "Thanks. My dinner items were down to canned or frozen. I didn't feel like either."

"I got milkshakes, too," he smiled. "But I had to drink them both on the way. They were getting too warm."

"That's fine. Means we don't need dessert."

Rick had already consumed half of his food by the time I got started on mine.

"Tell me what you know so far," he said.

"This is all *off the record.*"

"Remember who taught you the importance of what that means," Rick said. "Now tell me what you know that we can't print, yet."

Chapter Twenty-Three

Rick ran the piece about Anne the next day. We agreed to drop a by-line, which simply means no one would know who authored the article. I fleshed out a story about a woman who had worked with one of the serial killer's victims. I also pulled in a few paragraphs about the SLC burning victim, and the two similar unsolved murders in New Mexico. I completed the story describing how Anne had been shot and killed, and in summation tied the story to New Mexico using the link that they were all murders without suspects, without witnesses, without endings.

I obtained an old photograph of a youthful Anne, a ninth grader, from her high school in Salt Lake City. This photo appeared with the piece.

Rick phoned a few days after the story ran to inform me he'd received more *letters to the editor* in regards to that piece than any other story that had ever appeared in his newspaper.

"What is their general theme?" I asked, referring to the reader's concerns.

"They want to know if the same person killed all these women. They want to know why he shot Anne. They want to know why he hasn't been caught."

"Interesting," I said.

"That's exactly what you wanted," Rick said. "Am I right?"

"Yes."

"What's your angle?"

"The cops will let this case fall to the bottom of the pile unless the public demands they stay with it, solve it, get this guy off the streets. People don't like knowing a serial killer is out there. Mayors and governors don't like it when the people all get upset at once."

"Chalk another one up for the news media," Rick said.

* * *

I wasn't sure what my next move would be.

Wasn't sure I had one.

Rather than allow myself too much time to send all this chatter back and forth through my mind, undoubtedly a stress producing activity, I phoned the galleries in Old Town. The gallery owners helped me comprise a list of which pottery items they'd sold out of, and I promised I'd bring a new inventory within the next few days.

After spending two full days throwing pots and firing them in the kiln, I loaded my car and headed for Albuquerque. Bailey was not pleased, but I made her accompany me. She buried her face in the air conditioner vent next to the passenger seat.

Both galleries had cats who lived there. Employed to handle rodent problems, they were paid with a soft cushion in the window and a terminally full bowl of kitty kibbles. Bailey knew these cats and always wanted to give them a good sniffing and a face washing. This day was no different, and helped my furry friend forget her grievances at being made to accompany me, instead of staying home to play with the neighbors.

"She's getting more gray hair," Sally, a gallery owner, noted.

"Yes," I sighed. "One of the reasons I've had to start supervising her a bit more. She's not pleased with the new restrictions."

"You remember my Snoops," Sally said.

"Your big yellow cat. I do miss the Snoops."

"He enjoyed his mornings. I always let him go out and check the Old Town Square. I knew he was getting up there in years and he didn't pay attention like he should. I knew I needed to stop the morning outings. An unleashed dog killed him right out there." She pointed through the window, across the street, toward a large oak tree.

"That must've broke your heart," I said.

"I cried for two months," she said.

"Don't know what I'll do when Bailey crosses over," I said. "Don't even want to think about that day. I'd like to never have that day."

"Just take good care of her and when the time comes you'll have great memories."

"This is true," I said. "And now, we need to direct ourselves homeward."

Bailey had settled down beside the gallery cat and did not want to get up.

"You can stay, then." I winked at Sally and began walking out the door, down the sidewalk. By the time I reached my car, Bailey was beside me wagging her tail.

"Changed your mind?" I asked.

The wagging tail and happy eyes suggested she'd forgiven me. I scratched her head and opened the door. In she jumped. I hurried to the driver's side and started up the engine, setting the air conditioner at *high*.

For a treat I stopped at an ice cream shop and bought myself two scoops of German chocolate. I bought Bailey two scoops of French Vanilla, her favorite.

During our drive home my mind kept tripping back to Flannery. I wondered if he'd seen the article about Anne. If he had, I was curious how he reacted, especially to that photograph of the young girl who'd caught his attention and possibly brought to surface his psychopath self. Of course, that was not her fault. She could have never owned guilt over what he made of himself.

Late afternoon during the end of August falls around six o'clock. It was late afternoon when I pulled into my carport and let Bailey out to run around. She was eager to read the day's history left on each rock and blade of grass in the yard.

"You not going to find Ben?" I asked. I'd already noted Mule was nowhere around. Odd. Mule was almost always near the house, especially after I'd been gone for a few hours. And Bailey rarely missed the opportunity to race off with one purpose: to locate Ben.

"Woof!" Bailey suddenly jumped back from the patio chair she now sniffed.

"What is it?" I asked. My neighbors left no scent. Bailey didn't bark at animal odors. She alerted at strange human smells. I could count Dunlap out. He'd still be here. I could count Shaw out, he always left his card on my patio table beneath a flower pot. I could count Rick out. He left notes, usually stuck in the screen door.

I never wore the holster into town. Instead I slipped the Beretta inside my handbag. Opening the zipper, I grabbed the pistol and released the safety. I tried my kitchen door. Locked. Walking the full perimeter of my house and all the out buildings, I checked every window and door. All locked. Nothing tampered with. There were no footprints. Unfortunately, my gravel driveway did not show tracks and a person could park in the driveway, walk along pavers to the patio, all without leaving tracks there, either.

Moving away from the driveway in the direction of Dana's adobe I spotted footprints. I dropped to my knees and examined them. Compared to my size eight, these were much wider and longer. I guessed the classic athlete's shoe track to be a man's size ten wide.

Had to be Flannery.

Athletic shoes were not going to serve him well in this wilderness. I wondered if he was driving a car. Of course he was driving a car. It'd be a rental obtained with stolen identification.

If Dana were here she'd call Shaw. She'd absolutely press trespassing charges, then she'd ask for repair reimbursement from Flannery for her fence. I dialed Shaw after I checked the adobe, the studio, and all the outside storage sheds at Dana's.

"I'll have the sheriff's office send a deputy out," Shaw said. "What can you establish he's interested in?"

"He's not interested in my houses, or out buildings. He walked around Dunlap's box trailer three times but he didn't open it."

"You don't know it's Flannery. I'm inclined to think it's not. Flannery would've been more aggressive. My guess is he'd have broken into one or both of your houses."

"No," I said, " it's him."

"Remember, Roscoe Flannery took vacation from his job. He doesn't know he lost that job and he has no idea he's a suspect in anything. In his mind he's still the predator, not the hunted."

"Your point is?" I asked.

"Flannery isn't desperate, and he still thinks he makes all the rules."

"Send the deputy." I hung up.

Just like a cop. He was adamant I get hold of him if I suspected Flannery found this place. I knew Flannery had been here, but now Shaw skated across my concern. Why ignore the homes and structures? Because these weren't related to Dunlap. Flannery did not miss those early television reports after North was killed, the ones revealing Dunlap was a truck driver. The box trailer belonged to a very large truck. I was glad Dunlap removed the license plate. It would be impossible to know who owned it. Flannery had no way of knowing the box trailer didn't actually belong here. He didn't know how many people lived here. Two homes, both apparently in use, he'd assume more than one person resided here, possibly two families. He would not draw unwanted attention to himself by tampering with these homes or out buildings. But his curiosity about the trailer would be too much. He'd inspect the box.

When the deputy arrived I retraced my route. The deputy agreed with Shaw. Nothing had been disturbed therefore there seemed to be no reason for my upset.

"Tourists use these rural roads a lot this time of year," the deputy said. "People are winding up vacations because school begins in another week. Probably just someone interested in the area. May have had a flat tire, wanted to use your telephone. Cell phones don't work around here, so they'd look for a house with a land line."

"Thanks for coming out," I said.

The deputy had noticed my sidearm. "You know how to use that pistol?" he asked.

"Yes."

"If this was a prowler, I'd be more worried about him than you. Call us if he returns."

The deputy offered half a smile and gave me one of his cards. I offered him a glass of lemonade, but he had another call to respond elsewhere in the county. I watched him drive away.

Now what?

Wait!

Ben missing.

Mule nowhere to be seen.

This began to add up. I knew Ben would never forget what Flannery looked like, and now I had a pretty good idea he saw my visitor this day. Ben took Mule because he believed Flannery to be some kind of evil source of bad events. Mule was beyond ever being harmed by a person, but Ben would not allow Mule to be disrespected.

He'd be somewhere with his menagerie. I guessed he was in the cave. After changing into my serious boots and donning a wide brimmed hat, I called Bailey and the two of us headed toward the cave. While we walked late afternoon settled over Northern New Mexico and the heat began to lift due to increasing cloud coverage. Monsoon rains were forecast and I could estimate by the low heavy clouds the air would be dense with rain by night fall.

"Woof!" Bailey announced she'd discovered the neighbors soon as she disappeared inside the cave. I trailed by a few minutes. When I reached the opening I peered in. Ben asked for candles a few days earlier. I discovered why. He'd placed them all across the cave's entrance, where they flickered each time a breeze flared. I stepped over the little flames and observed Ben, Mule, the polar bears, Rooster, and the Happy Hens. Bailey joined them at the back of the cave.

"What's with this?" I gestured toward the candles.

"The fire will make the bad man go away." Ben puffed with defiance.

"He was here," I said. "The bad man who shot your good friend Dunlap, he's back."

"I saw him sneaking around the club house."

"He knows that's Dunlap's trailer," I said. "He'll show up again."

"He can't come in here," Ben said. "Bad spirits can't cross the fire."

His little candle barrier seemed pitiful. "Ben," I said, "I want you to promise me something."

"Okay."

"If he does come back, and if he can see you, or Mule, or your polar bears, or Rooster, or the Happy Hens, I want you to play a game."

"Okay. What is the game?"

"I want you to pretend to be like you once were. A live little boy. Don't let him know our secret."

"I am an ancient," Ben smiled.

"You certainly are. But the bad man does not need to know this."

"Okay."

"And if I ask you to do something, you will not ask questions."

Ben smiled.

"You will not ask questions," I repeated, this time putting as much intention as possible in my words.

"Okay."

"The bad man wants to harm Dunlap," I said.

"I won't let him harm my good friend Corey Dunlap."

"That's the plan," I said. "And we must also protect Bailey."

Ben grabbed Bailey and gave her a bear hug.

"I'll head on home, now," I said. "Bailey, you come with me."

Reluctantly Bailey left the cave and joined me. During our trek to the house I wondered what might happen. I didn't want Flannery to understand anything about my neighbors. If he did end up in prison, my neighbors didn't need that kind of attention.

CHAPTER TWENTY-FOUR

Uneventful days continued to pass, right into autumn. I knew Flannery watched my property, I simply didn't know when. Forest between the houses and highway was dense which meant I could not see vehicles. The distance was also too far to hear what little traffic passed by.

"Myra!" Ben called from the yard.

I walked through the ceramic studio door and stepped outside. "What's up?"

"I need more candles."

"I gave you two boxes of candles," I said. Wiping clay off my hands I covered my current pottery project with a large plastic bowl. "Not sure I have any more."

"Dana has candles," Ben said.

"She used to have candles," I corrected.

"Can we look?"

I opened up the adobe and noticed it was acquiring the odor of an uninhabited home. Dust and uncirculated air caused the deserted smell. I threw up several windows. Dunlap hadn't visited in two months, which turned out to be a good thing considering the attention we'd had from Flannery.

"You were correct," I called out.

"Dana always kept candles everywhere," Ben skipped into the small living room.

I removed one of about ten boxes from a corner cabinet. Each box contained one dozen long burning candles. "If you only use six candles at one time," I explained, "you can place them across the cave entrance and let them burn down. Then use the other six. These will keep a flame for about twelve hours."

"Okay," Ben grabbed the box and disappeared into the hills.

Since Ben came up with the idea of using tiny torches to protect his sacred cave from Flannery, I guessed I'd purchased dozens of candles. I learned to select those similar to the kind Dana had stored with wide diameters. One candle could hold a flame for almost twelve hours.

Taking a seat on the small sofa, I pulled a few of the candles from a box and lit them. A vanilla aroma wafted into the air and I hoped this might rid the house of that scent of abandon. Odd how little things like this opened the door to so many memories. I would always be grateful my cousin found what remained of her family. If she hadn't searched for me and our niece, I'd have never known either of these remarkable people who shared my ancestry, and the three of us would've lived our lives as little sailboats adrift in a lonely sea.

"Excuse me." A man said.

I nearly jumped through my skin when I glanced up from the sofa to see Roscoe Flannery standing in Dana's living room.

"Hello." I forced calm but knew curious clouded my tone. "Can I help you?"

"Excuse me for entering without knocking. Your door was wide open. I've got a flat tire up on the highway. Saw this dirt road and decided to follow it, see if there was a house anywhere out here."

"You don't carry a spare?" I asked.

Flannery shrugged and flashed a perfect smile. "Not as prepared as I should be," he said. "If I could just use your telephone?"

"It's currently not working," I said. Dana's phone service actually wasn't on, and I didn't plan on taking this creep across the field to my house. I stood up and instinctively reached to the area where I should have my Beretta. I'd removed it while working with wet clay. Currently both pistol and holster were laying on a stool out in the studio. "I'm just taking a break," I added. "I'd offer to help you but I'm quite busy." Still wearing my clay and glaze stained smock, that would be obvious.

"Not to worry," he said. Flannery inhaled, as if he'd decided I was neither a witness nor a potential target. "Well, if your phone isn't working, I guess I'll have to use that temporary spare in my trunk."

"I've used those before," I offered. "They work just fine."

"I'm traveling north and I won't make it to Denver with a temp spare."

"Lot of small towns between here and Denver."

"I'll go back to Santa Fe."

"Probably a good idea," I said.

"Could I have a glass of water?" He was stalling and not entirely satisfied with what he'd learned so far.

I crossed the living room without turning my back to Flannery and rounded the corner, fetched him a glass of water from the kitchen faucet. He accepted the water and drank it all down before heading for the open doorway. I trailed a few yards behind. Once we were standing in the yard, Flannery used the opportunity to bring up Dunlap's box trailer.

"Nice truck trailer you've got there."

"Belonged to my ex-husband."

"Refrigerated." Flannery said this while staring at my fraudulent wedding ring.

"He hauled frozen food."

"Really? What happened to the truck?"

"Sold it," I said.

"Really? Why didn't you sell the trailer, too?"

Flannery was trying to trip me. "I use it for storage," I said. "So where did you say your car was?"

"About a mile from here."

I nodded and smiled, portrayed myself as uninterested in his plight and unworried about his identity. He'd run out of excuses to hang around and ask questions. He could see I wasn't going to be helpful. "I'd give you a ride back up the road, but as you can see," I held out the pottery smock, "I'm quite busy."

"Wouldn't want to bother you," he said. Then he glanced toward my house. "Nice home. Belong to your family?"

"Extended family." I'd let him think I didn't live here alone.

"Well, I don't want to keep you from your work," he said. "Thanks for the water."

I watched Flannery walk down my driveway and considered my options. I'd already asked Shaw for assistance. Shaw handed me off to a deputy, and the deputy thought Flannery needed to be more worried about me and my Beretta.

"He's back," Ben said.

I turned around and discovered Ben, Mule, Bailey, Rooster, the Happy Hens, and the polar bears. The bears crouched with Bailey behind Mule. Rooster and the Happy Hens perched precariously on Mule's back.

Polar bears in New Mexico would probably distract Flannery, if nothing else.

Ben and his menagerie followed while I secured the adobe, checked the ceramic studio, and then paced the full length of my dirt road out to the highway. I tracked alongside the road north and south, both sides of the pavement, until I discovered where Flannery pulled his rental onto the shoulder and parked. He wore the same athletic shoes he'd been wearing last time he visited my place. I wished I'd taken a photograph or made an imprint using plaster of the print during his first visit. I'd be able to prove Flannery was scoping out my property in search of a link with Dunlap.

"Dana would know what to do," Ben said sarcastically.

I nodded my head. He was correct.

"We should make a trap," Ben said.

"How would we do that?" My curiosity peaked.

"If he goes into the clubhouse, we can close the doors. We can keep him there until he dies." Ben grinned from ear to ear.

I had the sudden image of myself locked inside the box trailer. "He's more likely to put us in there than the other way around," I said.

I did not have any delusions that I knew where Flannery went when he left here, but I was reasonably sure he would be around awhile. He did not know Dunlap wasn't a resident of New Mexico. For all he knew, Dunlap lived and worked in the vicinity of Santa Fe.

"I better go check my candles," Ben said. Bailey and the menagerie disappeared with Ben.

Returning to the adobe, I dug out Dana's automatic light timer switches and set them to turn indoor lights on around eight in the evening, and off around midnight. The timers alternated, allowing lights to switch on or off thirty minutes in either direction, which created the illusion of a more realistic schedule.

After returning to my house I dialed Shaw's office number. His voice messaging picked up. I then dialed his various other phone numbers, and with each one all I heard were more voice messages. I wondered where Shaw was at, since he'd always quickly picked up one of his phones.

I left one message for Shaw.

"Flannery dropped by today. Reminded me of Haggis."

* * *

When Bailey didn't arrive home by bedtime, I grabbed a flashlight and hiked to Ben's cave. I found all the candles perfectly spaced and positioned toward the center of the cave, probably to keep a breeze from dousing his tiny torches. The effect stirred me and it did seem both sacred and ritualistic at the same time.

Ben was nowhere to be found.

Except for Bailey, who sat attentive, appearing totally bewildered, the cave was empty.

Did Ben leave her there because he believed she was protected behind the candles?

His abandonment of her after all I'd cautioned him about recently, left me puzzled.

"C'mon girl," I called to Bailey. She continued to sit there as if frozen in her position.

"Ben said you could not leave, didn't he?"

Bailey whined and groveled, her nose close to the cave floor.

"It's okay. Ben meant for you to remain until I came to get you. Let's go home."

She would not budge. I stepped across the torch barrier and stood over her. She fixed me with her large pooch eyes, her way of trying to tell me something.

"Unlike Ben," I said, "I cannot read your thoughts. Now, it's time to leave here."

When I stepped back across the flames my flashlight picked up something odd. Dropping to my knees I scanned the area more closely.

Flannery's foot prints approached the cave. Strange as it seemed, the tracks did not cross the tiny torch line. A thought hit the side of my head like a baseball bat.

"He isn't scoping out this area in search of Dunlap!" I said. "He's been searching for Ben! He saw Ben that night. While he forced Veronica into the trunk and struggled with Dunlap, when he shot Dunlap, somewhere during that chaos he saw the little boy who came out of nowhere."

With my flashlight I continued to examine the shoe tracks until my suspicions were solid.

Flannery could not pierce the barrier.

Based on impressions in the soil he tried to step across half a dozen times but obviously failed to pass through, which is why Bailey remained behind the candles in the hallowed cave.

Flannery believed he'd taken a child hostage.

Did the rest of the menagerie disappear? Or did Ben hide them behind an ancient veil? He would not allow Flannery to see his collection of other-world friends. Pollution of good by evil, that's what Ben would perceive and shield against.

I stepped carefully around the cave, touching rocks and earth, until my arm brushed past a warm spot. Unlike those tales which always imply ghosts are accompanied by cool sensations, a soothing warm feeling is present when one is near a Spirit.

I slowly waved my arm over the site again. Instantly the veil dropped revealing Mule, the polar bears, Rooster, and the Happy Hens.

"Ben hid you very well," I said.

I now knew what caused Bailey's bewilderment. Animals live in the present moment. They don't spend time fretting over what was or what will be. In that wink-of-an-eye a short while ago she was comfortably settled with Ben and all her friends. When Flannery showed up, Ben cast the veil which kept Flannery from seeing Mule and the others. Unfortunately, the veil also hid them from Bailey. She did not know what happened to her little family. Now, as abruptly as they'd disappeared, here they were back again. Her present moment was transiently disturbed. But, in true animal character, she directly forgot her confusion. All was right with her world again.

Together we all exited the cave and traipsed through the dark night towards the house.

* * *

What would Flannery do next and where the hell was Shaw? I asked this question over and over so many times in my mind I imagined the question became a physical part of my brain's deep limbic system.

Knowing nothing could harm Ben, I kept the Beretta beside my pillow. Bailey and all her friends slept in the den and I eventually drifted off for a few hours. At dawn I was awakened by two fluffy white bear cubs pouncing on my back. I'd been wrong. They did not have sharp claws. In truth, they seemed more like circus teddy bears. At the sound of their mother's *get back to momma right now* roar they scampered out the door and down the hallway.

When I entered my huge kitchen and den area it was obvious life would never be the same. Mule parked himself beside the large French doors which exited the den onto the patio. In the fashion he'd always enjoyed from the other side of the glass, he now spied on the outdoors. Rooster and the Happy Hens lined up along the top row of cabinets above the sink. The polar bears and Bailey lounged on my cool stone floor which stretched from the main doorway to my central counter.

For some reason, which more likely had to do with Ben, they all believed Flannery to be dangerous to them, as well. Here, indoors, they considered I'd be their protector. Ben shielded them before, and now they believed I was it.

While I rummaged around for coffee filters, Rooster jumped down from the cabinet and raced around the floor, first scratching, then watching me. He wanted chicken feed.

"You want treats, you can have them outside," I said. He shook his head tousle and flew back onto the cabinet. I dropped the idea of a nice peaceful quiet cup of coffee.

"How about we all take a nice walk up to the ruins," I said.

After a quick shower, I dressed in cutoff jeans and a light sweatshirt. Although September could be warm, today hinted a fast approaching autumn waited around the corner. Cool enough for a long sleeve top, but warm enough for shorts. I opened the kitchen door and coaxed Mule and Bailey to follow me outside, since they were usually up for a walkabout.

Mule slowly tore himself from his new post by the large glass doors. He plodded past the others and joined me on the patio. I adjusted his sombrero, then we began our trek across the field. By the time we were hiking over the hill Bailey and the rest of Ben's menagerie joined us. I pretended all our behaviors were normal. They weren't of course. I wondered where Sam and Kopeki, or even Nakani had been this past month. I'd tell them … "

"Where's Ben?" Sam asked.

I spun around to see both fossils tromping a few feet behind Mule, who was on my heels.

"Hey!" I think I'd never been so happy to see anyone. "Where've you been? My coffee pot and television miss you!"

"The other side doesn't run on one track," Sam said. "Where's Ben?"

A pine tree had fallen across a section of the trail here and I sat on it. "Ben has been kidnapped," I said.

Sam and Kopeki took a seat on either side of me.

"You can't capture an ancient," Kopeki said, grinning broadly.

"No," Sam agreed. "It'd be impossible to take our young Ben. He's an ancient."

"I'm not sure," I said, "but I think he's playing a game with the man who shot Dunlap. The serial killer. He's been to the house."

"And our Ben is up to some tricks?" Sam asked.

"Ben can be a very good trickster," Kopeki grinned and nodded.

I explained what happened when Flannery showed up at Dana's a few days earlier. I then carefully described the scenario in the cave, how Flannery could not cross the candle barrier, how Ben created some kind of drape which masked the animals, except for Bailey.

"Sounds like a pretty good shroud," Sam said.

"I'm a bit worried," I confessed. "Although I realize Flannery cannot harm Ben."

"Nothing to fret over," Sam assured. "Ben's as good a trickster as you'll find, when he wants to be. We'll just have to be patient. See what this Flannery fellow thinks he wants."

"He wants Ben and Dunlap. Those are the only two eye witnesses who can positively ID him as Veronica North's killer."

Both Sam and Kopeki shook their heads.

"I know," I said. "Flannery doesn't know that."

Sam inhaled deeply. "Some people, like this Flannery fellow, don't know how precious life is. They steal other people's time. Go around killin' folks like it don't matter. I reckon that Haggis rabbit could tell him a few things. Wouldn't make no difference. Them's twisted characters. Can't be fixed in their lifetime. Oh, they get fixed, for sure, but that'll come by and by. Ain't gonna get away from havin' to make payments later on all the wrong he's doin' now."

"I guess we just wait," I said. "Don't know what else to do."

"We'll take Ben's critters," Sam said.

I stood with Bailey and watched them continue walking toward the ruins. There wasn't much they could do to help, and I wouldn't expect them to try. Ghosts are like memories. They keep you company, entertain you, have lovely fireside chats with you, and then they vanish.

I decided to return home and give Shaw another call.

Chapter Twenty-Five

Locked doors and windows never kept anyone out of a home. Flannery could break glass or shatter a French door and be inside within seconds. I sat on the patio and practiced conscious breathing for ten minutes, then crossed the threshold.

After a morning hike during which I surveyed entry areas in search of an intruder, I'd returned home. Now I worried what I'd find inside. Armed with the Beretta, I did not need to worry about my safety, yet I had to comfort myself by checking every room, closet, and even beneath beds and sofas.

"All clear," I told Bailey. She helped me inspect the house, then asked to go back outside.

I picked up my telephone and dialed each of Shaw's numbers. Tired of voice messaging, I called the main office.

"Detective Shaw is home with the flu," the man said. "Something I can help you with?"

Not trusting that anyone else would take me seriously, I said, "No. Thank you."

So much for *Call me anytime.*

Scrambling an egg with cheese and green chili, and brewing some tea, I attempted to eat, but managed only a couple bites.

Daily routines such as breakfast drifted far from my focus. Flannery abducted Ben. Even though this was more a joke on Flannery than anything worrisome, I wondered what his angle would be.

From somewhere outside Bailey launched into frantic barking.

To keep them out of Flannery's hands, I'd stored my shotgun and hunting rifle in the gun vault inside my bedroom walk-in closet. Not wanting to take time to fetch a long barrel I grabbed the Beretta and raced across the field toward Dunlap's box trailer, which was the direction the barking came from. After searching all around it appeared things were as they should be. Unexpectedly my eyes picked up dark red stains on the soil. I got a closer look when I dropped to one knee.

Blood.

Two sets of foot prints, the larger disappeared into the trailer and did not emerge.

The smaller athletic shoe tracks were Flannery's.

Hurriedly I unlatched the trailer doors and threw them wide.

A man sprawled prone toward the front of the box.

"Detective Shaw?" I called out. Quickly I jumped inside and kneeled beside him, instinctively checking for a pulse.

Still alive. No visible blood on his back. Carefully I rolled him over, hoping my actions weren't making matters worse.

"Are the bears still here?" he whispered, trying to open his eyes.

"No bears, Shaw, just me."

"Who are you?" he asked.

"Myra Whitehawk. You've been shot. I'm not sure where. Front of your shirt is soaked with blood. I need to remove it."

"Rio Grande Zoo," he whispered. "We're in the bear's den. Roscoe Flannery's trapped us in here with the bears. They'll kill us and save him doing it. Don't matter," he shook his head and coughed. "We're just bear food. Don't matter." Shaw coughed again and tried to sit up.

"Be still," I said. It was impossible to tell if his cough came from the gunshot wound, or influenza. He had a fever and appeared to still be suffering with the worst of the flu. Removing his shirt I noted what appeared to be an entry wound into his right chest. "You're one lucky son-of-a-gun," I said. "Heart's on the other side. You've lost a lot of blood, but I don't hear any air escaping. I think that means your lung isn't punctured. Small hole adds up to small caliber. That's good, too, but the bullet fragment is still inside."

"Don't matter," he mumbled.

"Shaw. Pay attention. I've got to leave you here a few minutes. Gotta run across the field and call an ambulance and the state police."

"No need. Cop's already here."

"Don't move. Just stay still." I glanced toward the front of the box trailer. Ben kept a few candles stored in plastic bins, along with Kopeki's favorite sitting blanket. I grabbed Kopeki's blanket and covered his shoulders. Muddled speech suggested he was in shock. If his body temperature began to drop, he'd die from cardiac arrest.

Jumping down from the trailer I ran faster than I'd run since…well, since Haggis. When I reached the telephone in my kitchen there was a big new problem.

No dial tone.

No way to call for help.

Flannery cut my phone line within the time I'd left to investigate Bailey's barking and now. Flannery was here. Wait a minute! Where was Shaw's vehicle?

Not wasting another second trying to put this new puzzle together, I rushed to my car, drove around to the box trailer, and headed back inside for Shaw.

"Can you stand up?" I asked.

"I'll try," he replied, trying to focus on my face. "That you, Whitehawk?"

"It's me. You've been shot. I'm taking you to the hospital in Santa Fe."

Shaw struggled to his knees, then managed to make it to his feet. We were almost to the open doors when Flannery appeared. I pulled the Beretta from my belt and he drew his pistol. I fired first, he fired second. He missed. I aimed for his heart, but hit his left arm. He threw the doors shut and I heard him cursing while securing the latch.

"You okay?" Shaw asked.

"I'm fine. Flannery's hit in the left arm. Nine mil slug close range. He's in trouble."

"Yeah," Shaw chuckled. "He'll bleed to death or lose the arm."

"I'm gonna help you sit back down," I said.

"Pitch dark in here," he said. "Bears'll be back any time now."

I knew he'd seen the polar bears, but I wondered where. With the doors closed, there was absolutely no visibility. I felt my way to the front of the box trailer and climbed on top of Ben's plastic bins, released the vent which was above the refrigeration unit. A small stream of light and fresh air filtered inside. Digging into the bins, I located several candles and some matches. I lit the candles and placed them inside the large shallow tin cans Ben used to catch the melting wax. He did not want to make any messes inside Dunlap's trailer.

Through the glow of the candles, I could make out something else. These weren't put here by Ben, or Shaw, or me. Flannery planted them here. He knew who I was, and he'd done some research. Two pints of Jack Daniel's. He intended to lock me inside here where he assumed I'd die of suffocation after I drank myself into a stupor. I was sure he hadn't planned on Shaw.

"Hey!" Flannery screamed. "You hear me?"

"I hear you," I said. Shaw collapsed onto the floor and I draped Kopeki's blanket around his shoulders for a second time.

"Tell that cop I set his personal car on fire."

"Really?" I'd surmised Shaw was home with the flu when he eventually got around to hearing my messages. Shaw'd driven up here in his own vehicle. I hoped he wasn't fond of it.

"I shot that bastard right through the heart. He's gonna die. You're gonna die, too. Goddamn kid's already dead."

Flannery didn't know his anatomy very well, but I would not tell him he'd missed Shaw's cardiac muscle by more than a few inches.

"You killed the boy? How?"

"What the fuck did I just say?" Flannery screeched. His voice broke up. I imagined his current situation, knew he was losing blood, knew he was in severe pain.

"You said you burned the cop's car."

"You idiot! Figure it out!" His tone sounded weaker.

I remained silent, decided not to respond anymore. If Flannery torched Shaw's car nearby, as he would have had to do considering not that much time passed, the flames and smoke would bring forestry fire personnel and possibly county and state police. I also knew Flannery needed emergency medical help. My keys were all in my pocket, so he couldn't leave with one of my vehicles.

"Missy, this fella could sure use some refreshment," a voice spoke from behind me. I turned around to see both Sam and Kopeki seated beside Shaw. They'd helped Shaw sit, helped him lean his back against the side of the box trailer. The Jack Daniel's bottles were open. Kopeki drank from one. Sam shared the other with Shaw.

"Not as good as a cup of coffee," Kopeki flashed a toothless grin and winked.

"Figurin' you wouldn't need this," Sam held up the bottle, then handed it back to Shaw, who took another generous swallow.

"Can you open these doors?" I asked.

"We tried," Sam said. "He put some locks on 'em."

"Where's Ben?"

"Ben's up in the cave with Bailey and all the other critters," Sam said.

"That's a relief." I let my knees collapse and sat across from the three. Flannery believed he was almost home free. After tossing Ben in Shaw's trunk and setting the car on fire, he perceived there'd only be one more witness to worry about: Dunlap.

"You men from around here?" Shaw slurred his words.

"We're from right here," Sam said.

"You neighbors of Whitehawk?"

"I am an ancient," Kopeki corrected. "Sam is my friend."

"You seen them bears?" Shaw asked.

"Mighty fine lookin' animals," Sam smiled and nodded.

While they talked, Nakani appeared and squatted next to Kopeki. He handed her the bottle and she drank what remained.

"You an anshen, or a neighbor?" Shaw asked her. His speech suggested he was growing intoxicated.

"I am a potter." Nakani folded her arms across her chest and postured proud.

"Yah? Well, we always ushe pots. Thas nice." Shaw's words were growing incoherent.

I tore Shaw's shirt into strips and used it to plug the bullet hole in his chest.

"He's asleep," Sam noted.

"Thanks," I said.

"For what?"

"For getting all that whisky gone before I decided to go at it myself."

"Ben told us what was happenin'," Sam said. "We came right down to help."

"Where is Ben?"

"Probably keepin' his candles lit up in that cave."

"Did he mention what Flannery did with Shaw's car?"

"That he did," Sam nodded. "Said that bad fella pulled this detective's car onto one of them forest trails. Maybe a mile or less, headin' north-west."

At that moment we heard the low rumble and heavy track of a big truck in the driveway.

"Fire truck, Sam. I'll bet they saw the car fire."

"No," Sam said. "Car wasn't burned. He just left Ben in the trunk."

"He didn't have time," I thought out loud. "Probably thought he'd torch it later today."

We all sat in a hushed silence, wondering what would happen next. That moment was chased by the sound of a rifle. Soon a friendly voice called out, "Somebody in there?"

"Dunlap! Shaw's wounded!"

"These doors are locked," he yelled. "Hold on! I've got bolt cutters in the truck."

Within minutes the doors were wide open and Dunlap stood there with his trademark grin, as if all were right with the world and nothing could ever be too bad for long.

"What happened? I heard the rifle."

"I sensed something was wrong when I came down the driveway and saw your car over here. Pulled out my rifle and got ready. Sure enough, Roscoe Flannery showed his ugly head around the side of your house. I popped him."

"You killed him?"

"Tried to, but it's hard to sight with these glasses. Flannery was already on his knees. Looked like he wasn't going nowhere. I shot him in the thigh."

"Where is he?"

"I took that cap pistol away from him and left him in the dirt. He ain't travelin' no more. Somebody already took out his left arm."

"We have to get Shaw to the hospital," I said. Glancing toward Shaw I noticed all my neighbors had left and taken the empty whisky bottles.

Dunlap got a whiff of Shaw. "He's either dying or drunk."

"Booze was Flannery's contribution," I said. "Jack Daniel's is a fairly good anesthetic."

Using Kopeki's blanket, we carefully pulled Shaw out of the box and carried him the few feet to my car.

"You got your truck," I said, noticing the big Kenworth in my yard.

"What about Flannery?" Dunlap asked the obvious.

"We can tie him up and put him in the box trailer," I suggested. "Shaw's people can deal with him."

During the drive to Santa Fe I filled Dunlap in on the whole story.

Chapter Twenty-Six

State Police used a helicopter to locate Flannery's rental. Concealed by trees and brush, he left it well inside the gate leading to a long abandoned ranch site. Twenty two pairs of car keys were collected by the feds while searching his home in Salt Lake City. The assumption was clear. He saved souvenirs to remember his violent fiery coffins. Problem was, there were only seventeen documented crimes fitting this profile. Cold case files in all fifty states did not reveal similar offenses. I wondered about Canada and Mexico, but no one asked for my input.

Serial killers hoard mementoes. Roscoe Flannery's prize possessions were twenty two sets of keys. Unsolved mysteries. Sorrows without rest. Perhaps during his long life in prison, he'd fess up but I wouldn't hold my breath.

Between the keys and Dunlap's testimony, a judge sentenced Flannery to serve multiple life terms without parole. I was in the courtroom accompanied by my young neighbor. Ben veiled himself so that only Flannery could see him, and several times Ben did what young children will do. He made faces, stuck out his tongue and crossed his eyes every time Flannery glared at him.

New Mexico's death penalty had recently been reversed by the governor, which saved Flannery from a hasty retreat into his next life. I thought of the Haggis rabbit and knew his next life would not please him. For that, I regretted we'd lost the death penalty.

After Flannery's trial, Dunlap hooked up his box trailer to his new truck and headed for steady work hauling frozen freight on the West Coast. Shaw survived his gunshot wound, but nearly died from pneumonia. He had to spend a couple weeks in the hospital. I thought he'd retire, but he didn't.

For me, life simply carried on.

* * *

"You finalizing that piece yet?" Rick asked soon as he arrived. Mule followed him in.

I grabbed a bucket of sweet molasses and grain treat off the counter and coaxed Mule back out to the patio.

"He's spying on us," Rick said. Mule peered through the large bay window.

"That's what he does," I smiled.

"Why's he still wearing that sombrero?"

"He likes it," I said.

"In December?"

"December, July, all the same to Mule."

Rick removed his coat and thermal gloves and tossed them on a chair in my den.

"I'll be fifty years old in a few years," I said, "and you'll be sixty five. How'd we get this old and end up always spending our holidays counting solitaire decks?"

"Hey," Rick said. "We're not alone. It's Christmas and we're sharing a nice meal of … what are you cooking?"

"Tamales, frijoles and sopapillas."

"You see? It's Christmas and we're not alone. We're sharing a damn good dinner."

"You drove all the way up here to bug me about those fluffy history pieces, not to share Christmas dinner."

"I'm publishing my New Year's magazine," Rick protested. "I need two good New Mexico historicals. You're the gal, Myra. You write great historicals."

"Set the table."

"Hey." Rick paused while pulling bowls and plates from a cabinet. "You heard Flannery lost that arm?"

"I did not hear. Surprised Shaw didn't phone. He called last month to wish me a happy Thanksgiving. He's still insisting he saw polar bears in Dunlap's box trailer. Said he knew later he was hallucinating about being trapped in the zoo, but swears he saw those bears."

"Shaw saw polar bears. Flannery says he locked a little boy in Shaw's car trunk. Must've been something in the air that day. Only thing in Shaw's trunk was a UNM Lobo cap."

"What happened?"

"I wasn't here, remember?"

"I mean, what happened to Flannery's arm?"

"You're the one who shot him."

"Yeah. But that was two months ago."

"Bone wouldn't heal. Picked up an infection."

"Humerus," I said.

"Okay?"

"Long bone in his arm. That's the one that shattered. So they took it off at the shoulder?"

"Gotcha. Say, do you think he'd have ever stopped?"

"No."

"Why?" Rick asked.

"He couldn't stop until someone stopped him. Oil is hot. You wanna toss the sopas in?"

Rick fried and turned the delicate bread, then allowed them to lose the excess oil while basking in a tray lined with napkins.

"Two tamales?" I asked.

"Three."

"Hand me your plate."

I dished up tamales and sopas, added a bowl of frijoles and green chili, and poured flutes of ginger ale over crushed ice.

"A Christmas dinner to make Dana proud," I said. "She's the one made me learn how to cook all this stuff."

Rick held his ginger ale into the air. I touched my glass to his.

"Cheers to Dana," we both said in unison.

In keeping with tradition, Rick talked me into writing two extensive historical articles for his New Year's magazine. And, in keeping with tradition, I watched the red taillights disappear down my driveway when he left for home later that evening.

Bailey snored softly from her cushion beside the fireplace in the den. I did not disturb her while I slipped on my parka and a pair of Dana's cozy fleece lined gloves. I hiked easily over the grounds where the old ruins rested peacefully. And because a bright moon guided me onward, I continued my trek across the hills where Rudy and Mule showed me the perfect place to liberate Dana's ashes into the wind.

When I found the boulder, I climbed to the top and sat holding my knees next to my chest. I could not recall ever seeing such glorious star formations in the Heavens. After a few moments I pulled off my old wedding ring and threw it into the darkness. It served a purpose, even if only to temporarily tilt Flannery's focus. Time to liberate that old broken circle.

Refreshed and renewed, I inhaled deeply and held my breath, then let it go.

The night air held the sweet chill of serenity.

After a short while one of the stars dropped from the sky settling next to me. In another moment a second star descended in a spray of twinkling light.

The Spirit Wolf leaned heavily against my side.

I draped an arm across his shoulders.

"I've missed you, my friend. I just wish Dana were here with us."

"I told you I would never be far away." Dana materialized from shimmering star dust, holding a large piece of pottery in her hands.

"Merry Christmas, Cousin," I said.

"Merry Christmas, Myra." She handed me the exquisite bowl which I held out to examine in the moonlight.

Painted with unique perfection, a bulky white bear and two cubs slept in deep snow.

From a place we cannot understand.

From a universe beyond the Black Holes of myth.

Where buffalo still run free.
Bring on the Ghost Dance.
There is infinity and perfect peace.
And we will live again. We will live again.

About the Author

Joan Leslie Woodruff has a Bachelor of Science Degree from Loma Linda University of Medicine and Allied Health Professions, Loma Linda, California. She is a Board Certified Occupational Therapist, Registered. Joan also has a postgraduate degree with double majors in Education and Counseling from California State University. Her career included supervising staff, directing departments, primary patient care, teaching interns, and setting up new clinics for hospitals around Southern California. Joan had the honor of being the first president of the Inland County Chapter of Occupational Therapists in Southern California. Her professional articles were frequently featured in journals for therapists and mental health workers around the country.

Joan's maternal and paternal families included Shawnee, Eastern Cherokee, German, and Russian ancestry. She was born on a USAF base in New Mexico and has traveled throughout the world several times. She has lived in New Mexico, Newfoundland, Tennessee, Arizona, and California. She currently lives on a ranch near the Anasazi ruins of Abo, New Mexico.

Joan's short fiction and nonfiction work has appeared around the country in both literary and commercial magazines. Her books include TRA-

DITIONAL STORIES AND FOODS; NEIGHBORS; THE SHILOH RENEWAL; GHOST IN THE RAINBOW; WISHES AND WIND-MILLS; and most recently, POLAR BEARS IN THE KITCHEN. Favorable reviews for her writing have appeared in newspapers, magazines, and online websites. Her books can be ordered through any bookstore, or purchased from hundreds of online bookstores all around the world.

Made in the USA
San Bernardino, CA
17 July 2020